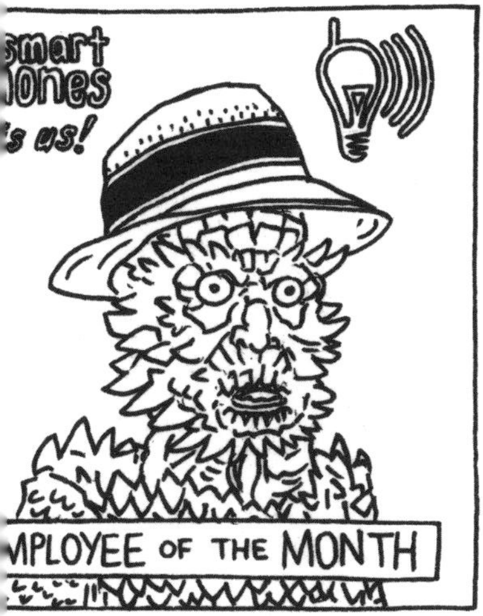
smart
ones
'S us!
MPLOYEE OF THE MONTH

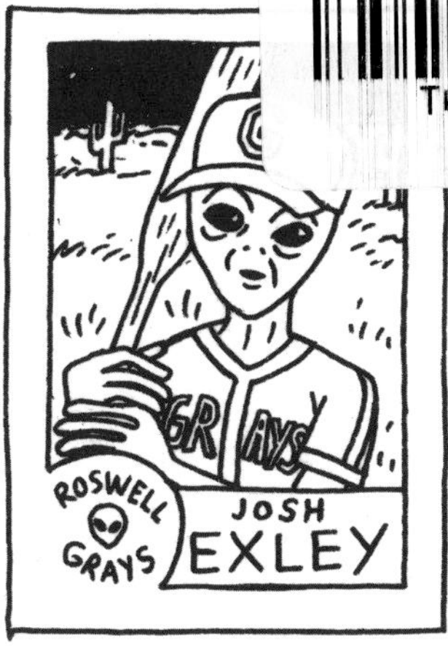
ROSWELL GRAYS
JOSH
EXLEY

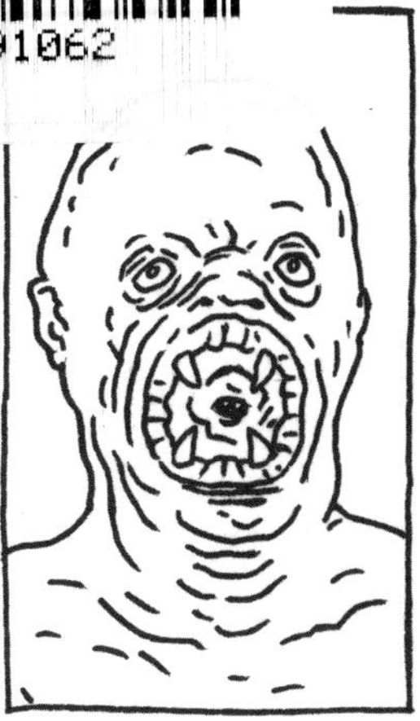

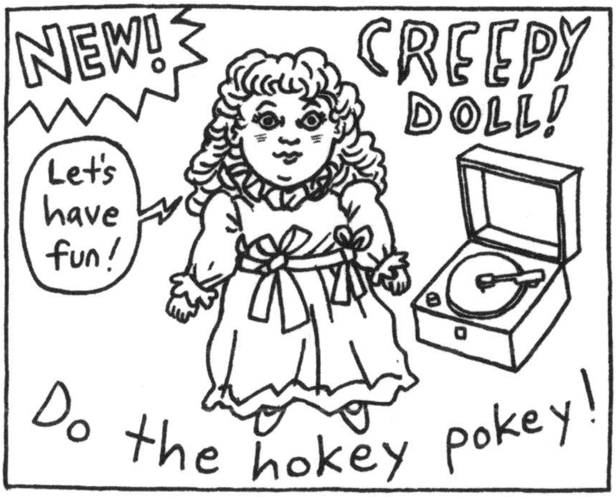
NEW!
CREEPY DOLL!
Let's have fun!
Do the hokey pokey!

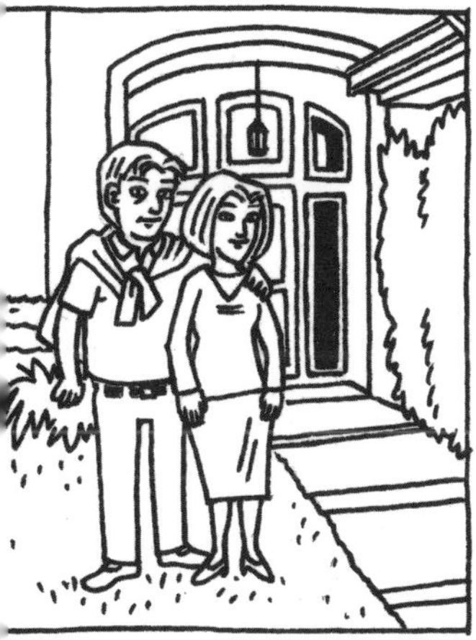

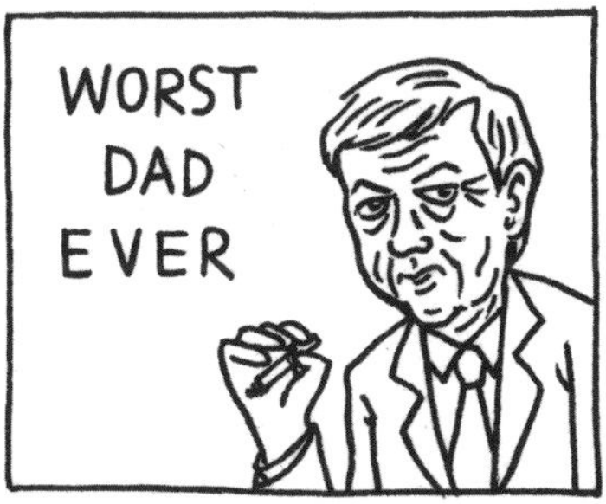
WORST DAD EVER

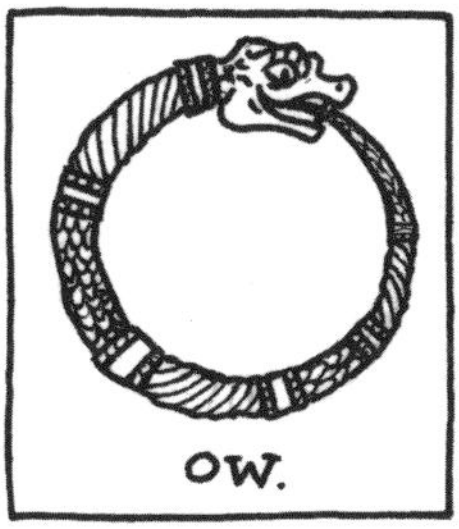
OW.

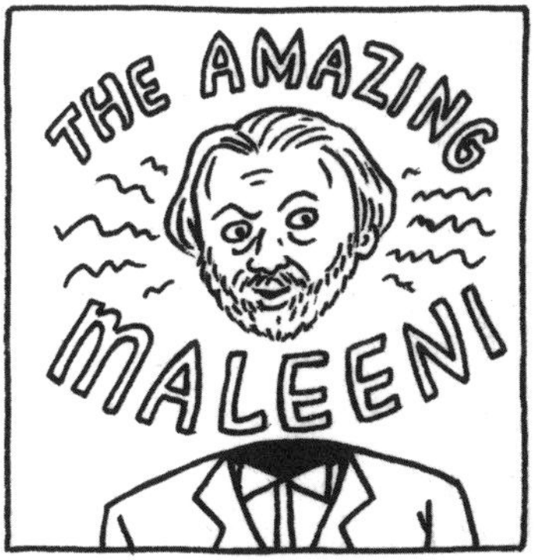
THE AMAZING
MALEENI

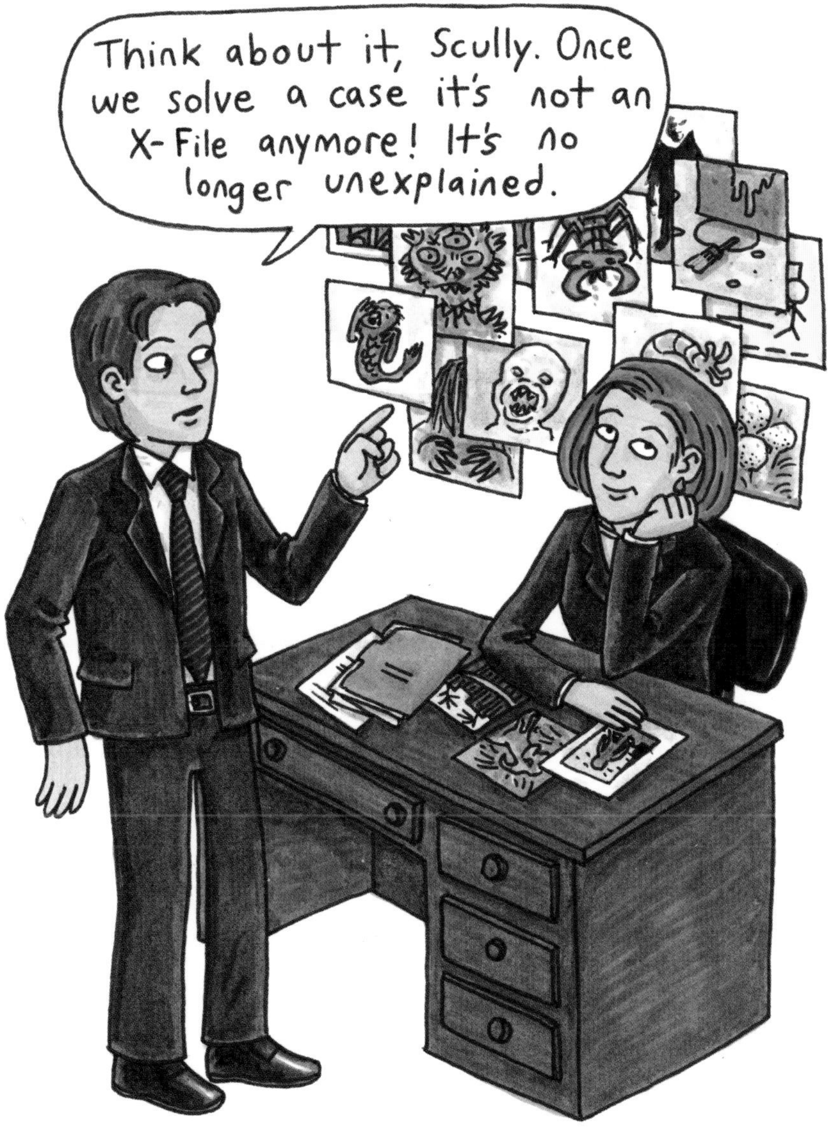
Think about it, Scully. Once we solve a case it's not an X-File anymore! It's no longer unexplained.

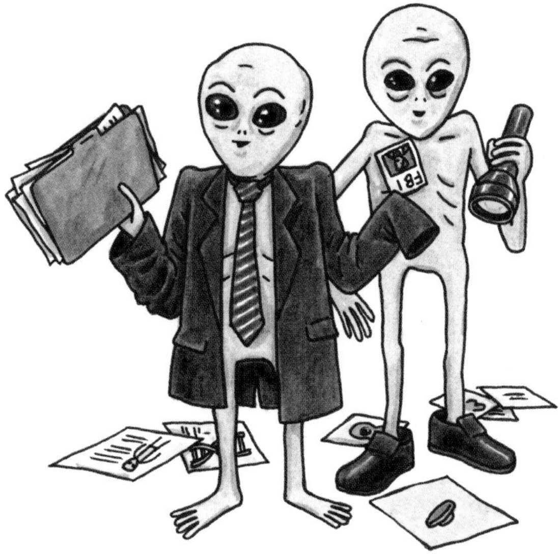
FBI

THE eXtra FILES

THE HUMOR IS OUT THERE.

JEFFREY BROWN

HYPERION AVENUE

LOS ANGELES • NEW YORK

Published by Hyperion Avenue, an imprint of Buena Vista Books, Inc. No part of this book may be reproduced or transmitted in any form or by any means, electronic or mechanical, including photocopying, recording, or by any information storage and retrieval system, without written permission from the publisher. For information address Hyperion Avenue, 77 West 66th Street, New York, New York 10023.

First Edition, November 2023
10 9 8 7 6 5 4 3 2 1
FAC 073226-23257
Printed in the United States of America

This book is set in Century Gothic Pro
Written and drawn by Jeffrey Brown

Library of Congress Cataloging-in-Publication Data on file.
ISBN 978-1-368-08431-4
Reinforced binding

www.HyperionAvenueBooks.com

SUSTAINABLE FORESTRY INITIATIVE

Certified Sourcing

www.forests.org
SFI-01681

Logo Applies to Text Stock Only

References to this skull-headed figure have appeared throughout mythology, even appearing in American comic books. My theory is this person - calling themself "Skully" - may have some biogenetic mutation and has infiltrated the FBI to -
Here, Mulder. You might want to look over the file on your new partner.
FOX MULDER

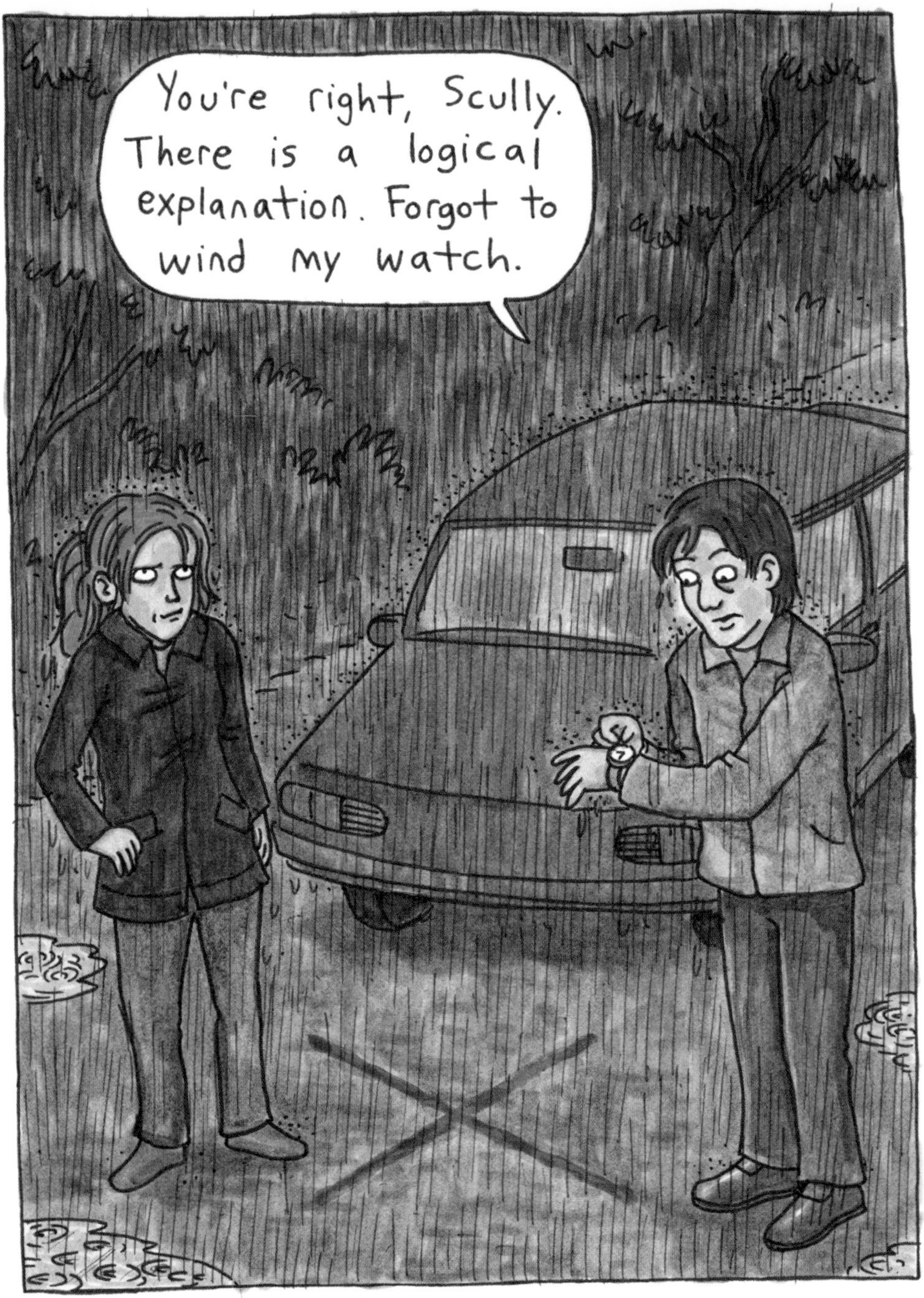
You're right, Scully. There is a logical explanation. Forgot to wind my watch.

PILOT

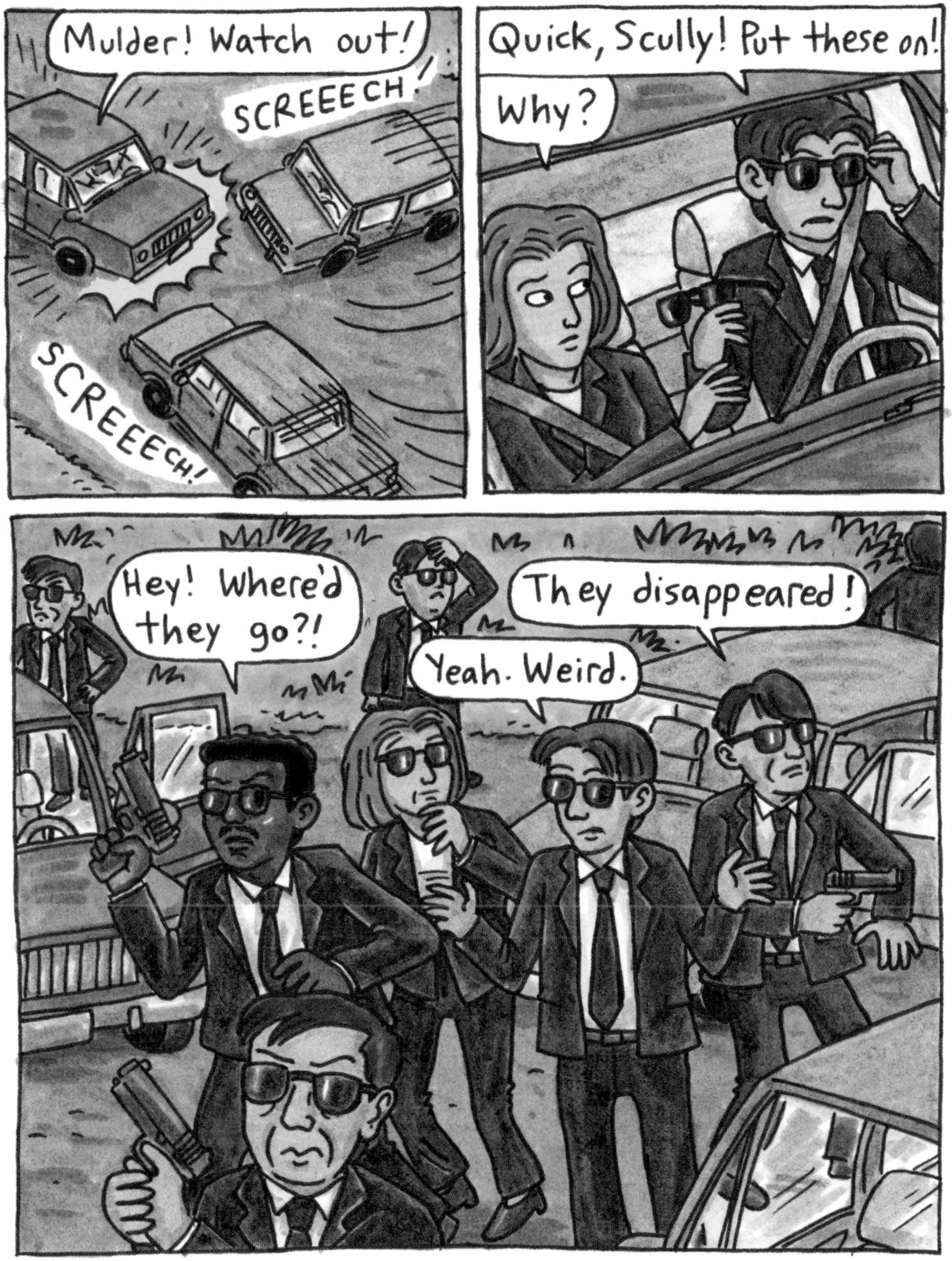
Mulder! Watch out!
SCREEECH!
SCREEEECH!
Quick, Scully! Put these on!
Why?
Hey! Where'd they go?!
They disappeared!
Yeah. Weird.

DEEP THROAT

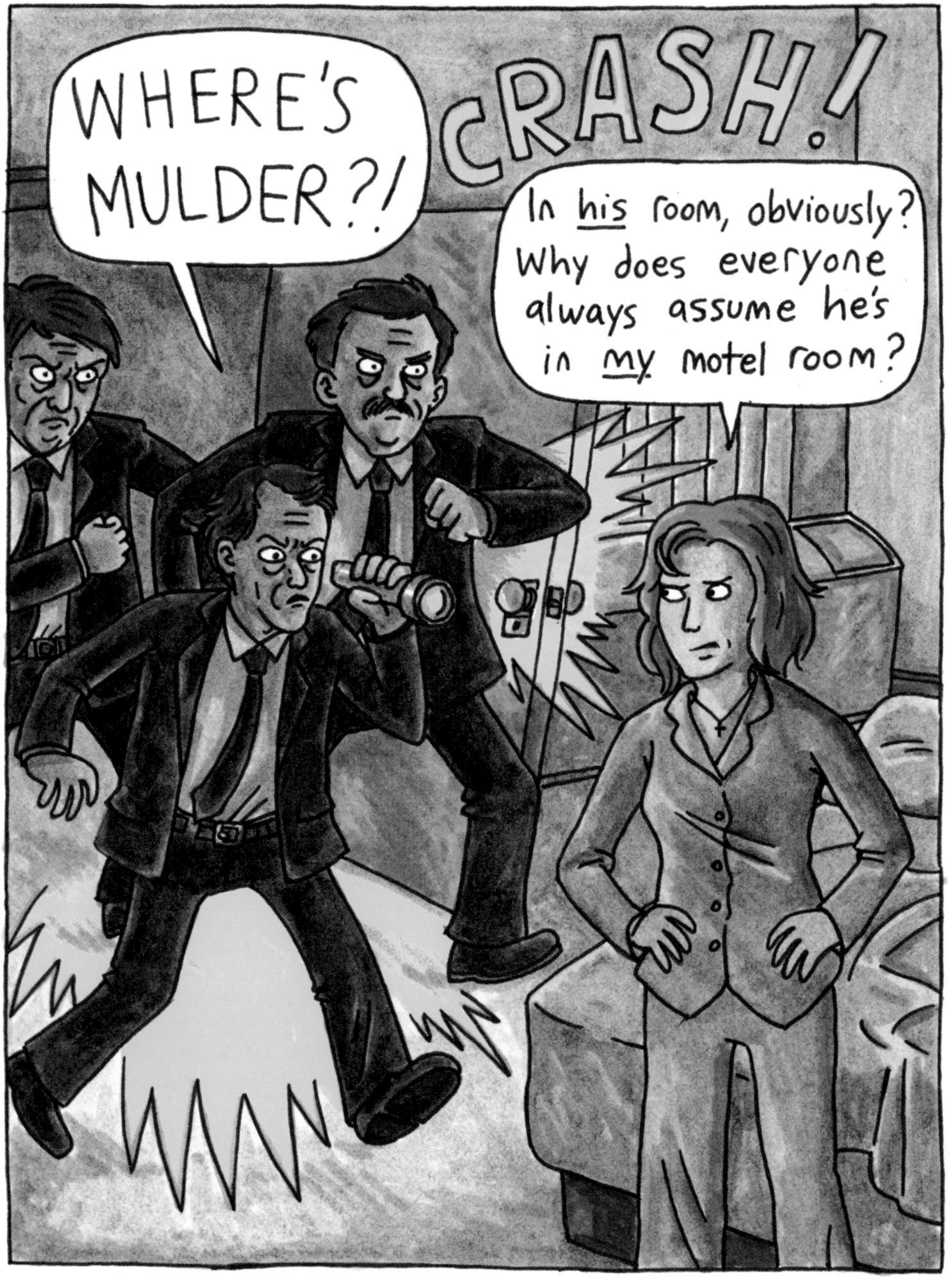
WHERE'S MULDER?!
CRASH!
In his room, obviously? Why does everyone always assume he's in my motel room?

CONDUIT

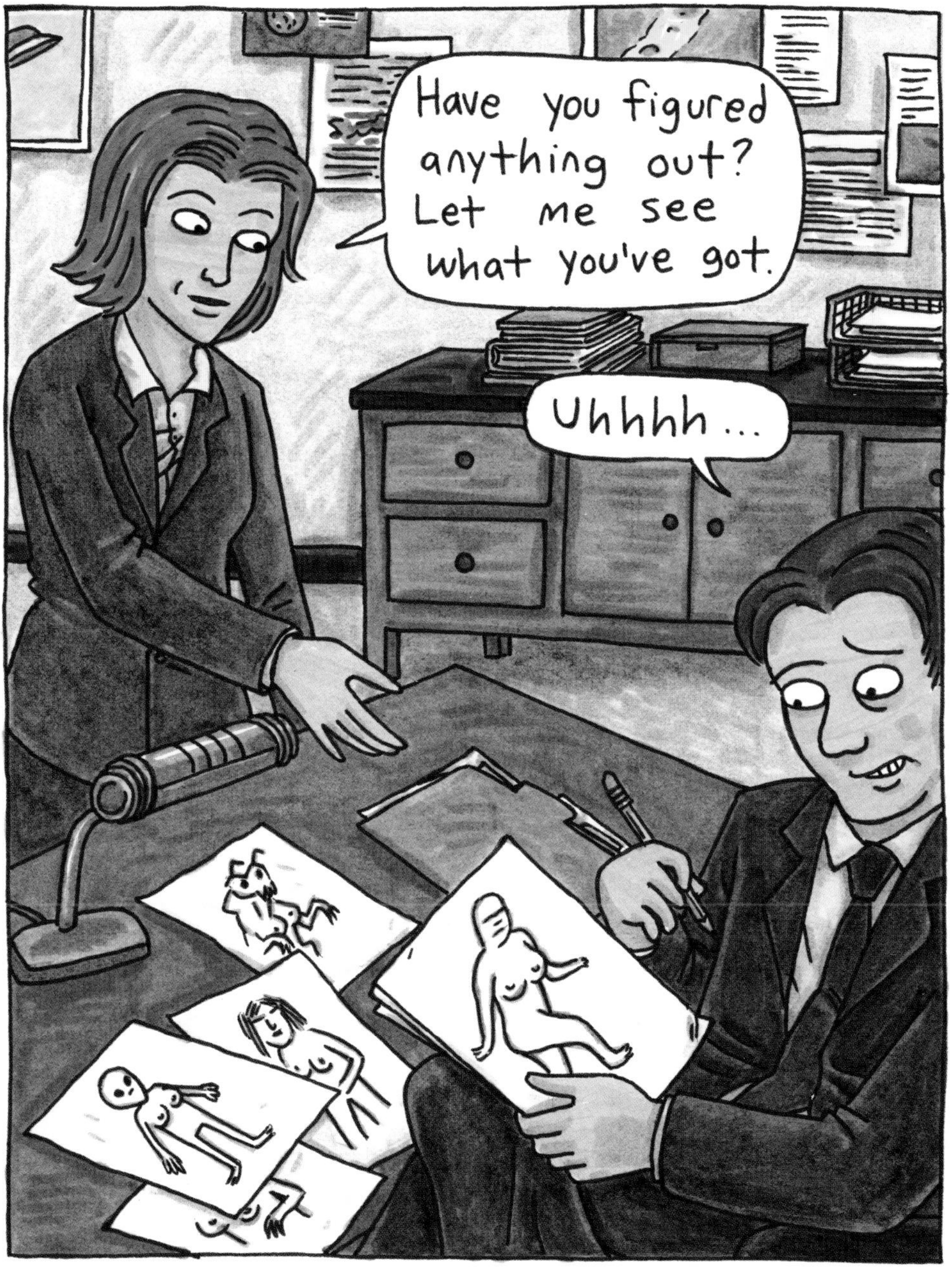
Have you figured anything out? Let me see what you've got.
Uhhhh...

THE JERSEY DEVIL

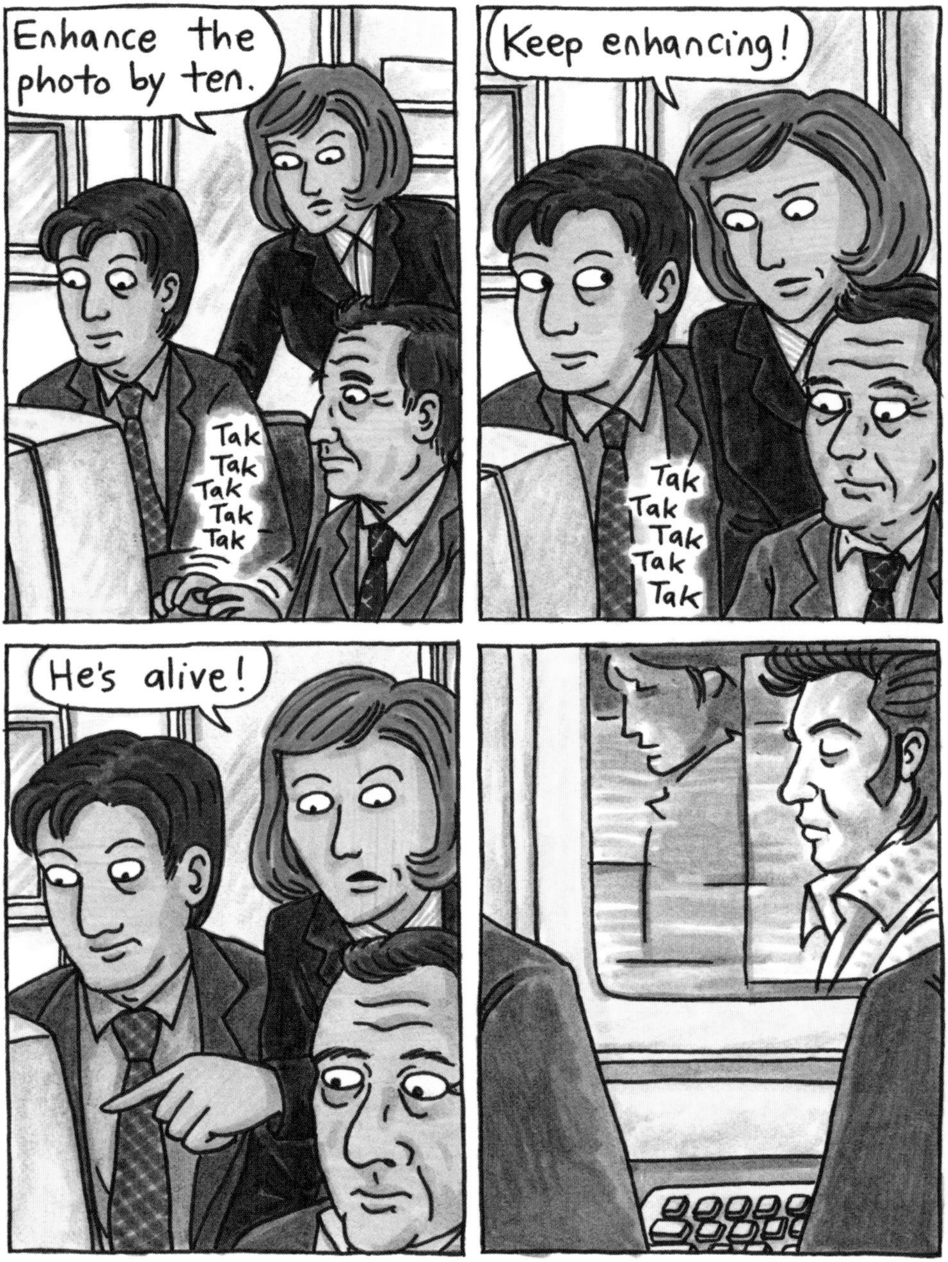
Enhance the photo by ten.
Tak Tak Tak Tak Tak
Keep enhancing!
Tak Tak Tak Tak Tak
He's alive!

SHADOWS

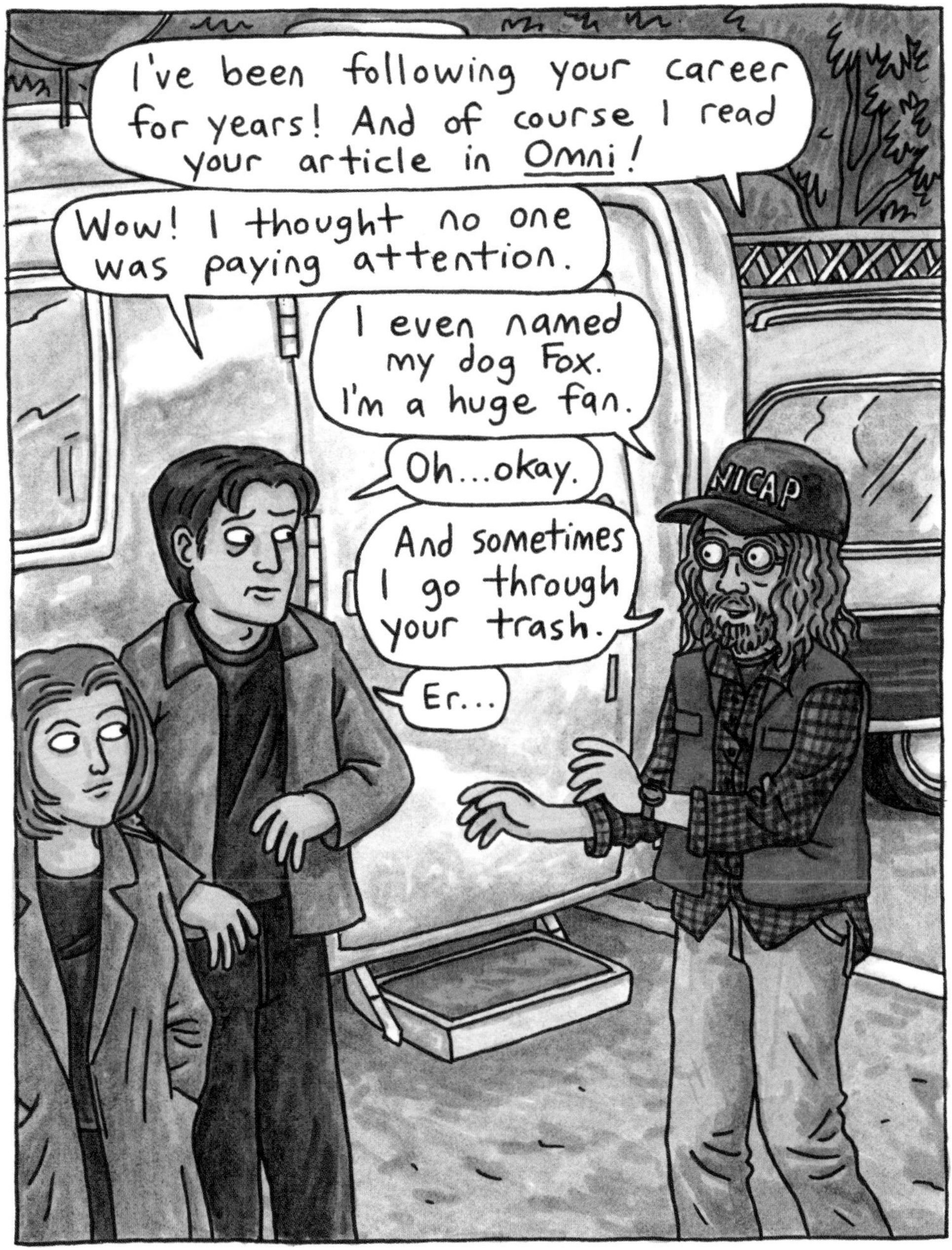
I've been following your career for years! And of course I read your article in Omni!
Wow! I thought no one was paying attention.
I even named my dog Fox. I'm a huge fan.
Oh...okay.
And sometimes I go through your trash.
Er...
NICAP

FALLEN ANGEL

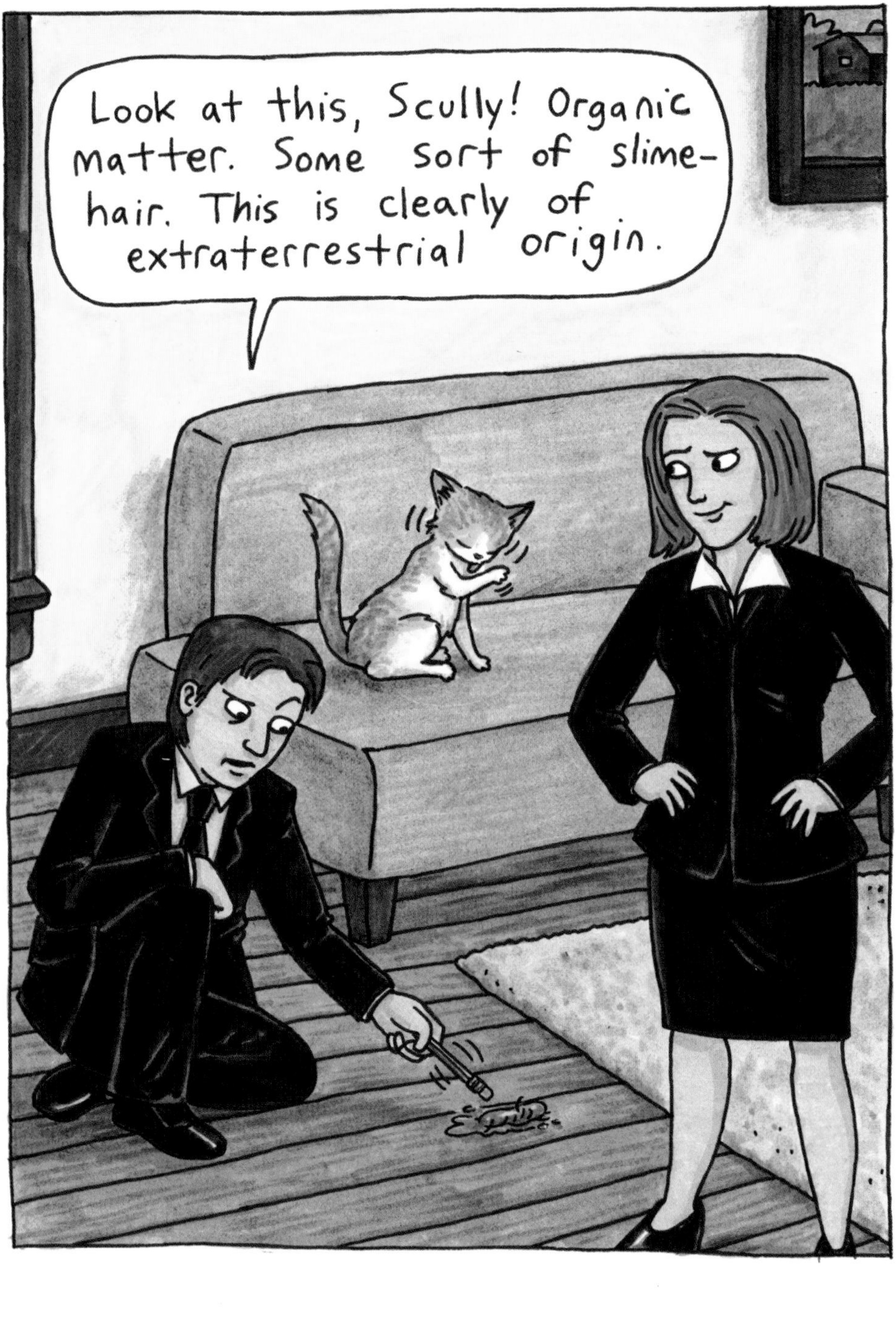
Look at this, Scully! Organic matter. Some sort of slime-hair. This is clearly of extraterrestrial origin.

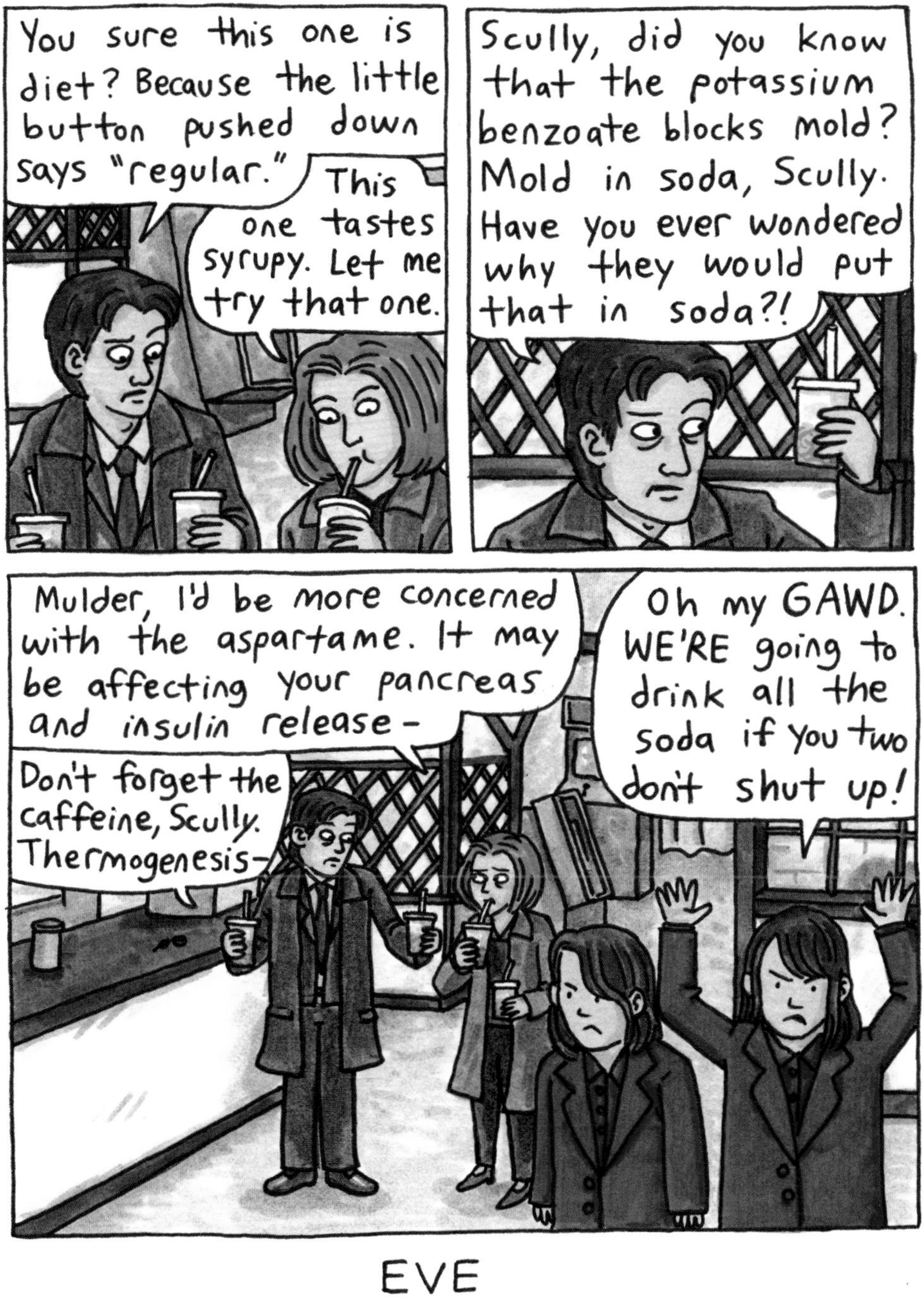
You sure this one is diet? Because the little button pushed down says "regular."
This one tastes syrupy. Let me try that one.
Scully, did you know that the potassium benzoate blocks mold? Mold in soda, Scully. Have you ever wondered why they would put that in soda?!
Mulder, I'd be more concerned with the aspartame. It may be affecting your pancreas and insulin release-
Don't forget the caffeine, Scully. Thermogenesis-
Oh my GAWD. WE'RE going to drink all the soda if you two don't shut up!

EVE

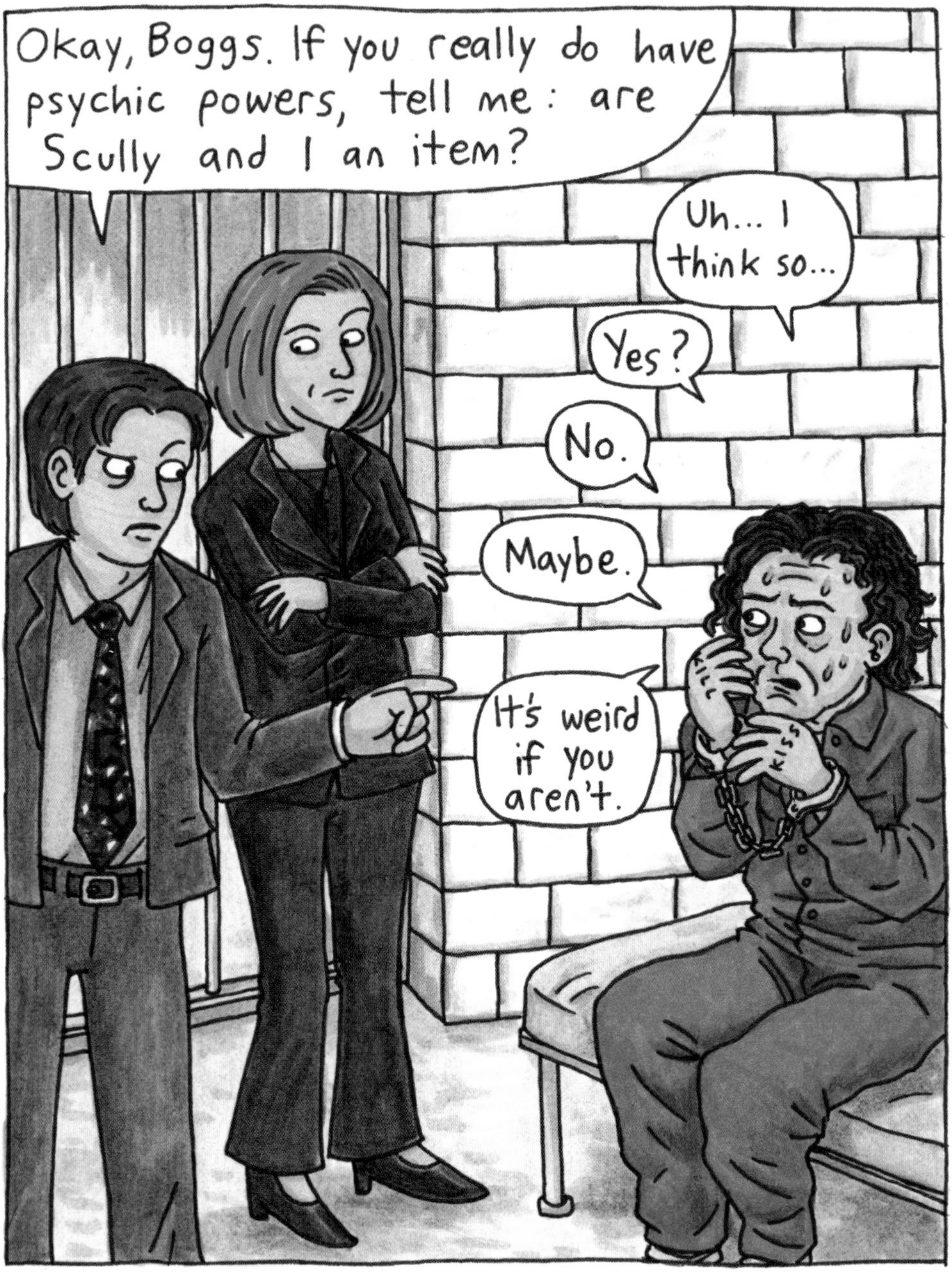
Okay, Boggs. If you really do have psychic powers, tell me: are Scully and I an item?
Uh... I think so...
Yes?
No.
Maybe.
It's weird if you aren't.

BEYOND THE SEA

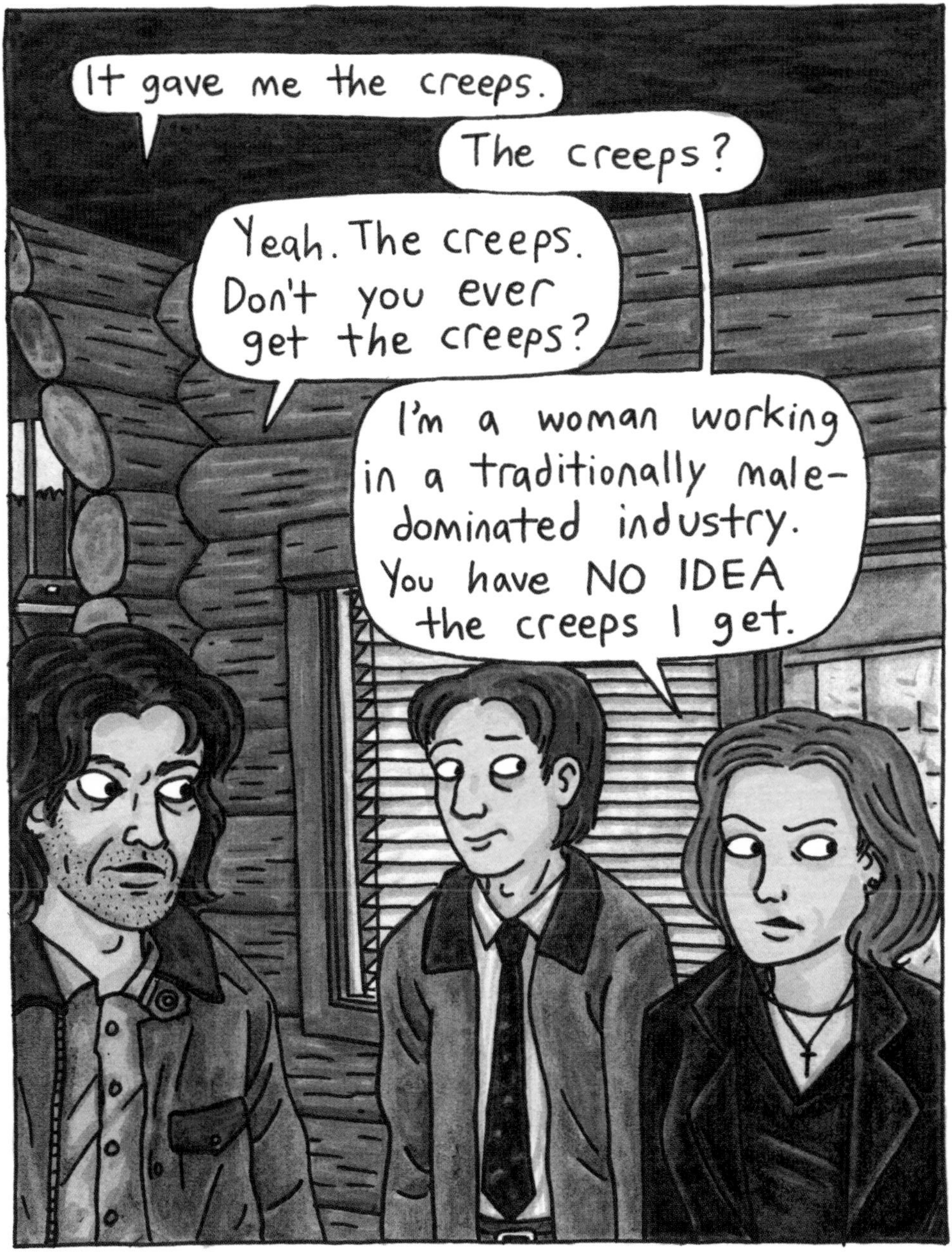
It gave me the creeps.
The creeps?
Yeah. The creeps. Don't you ever get the creeps?
I'm a woman working in a traditionally male-dominated industry. You have NO IDEA the creeps I get.

SHAPES

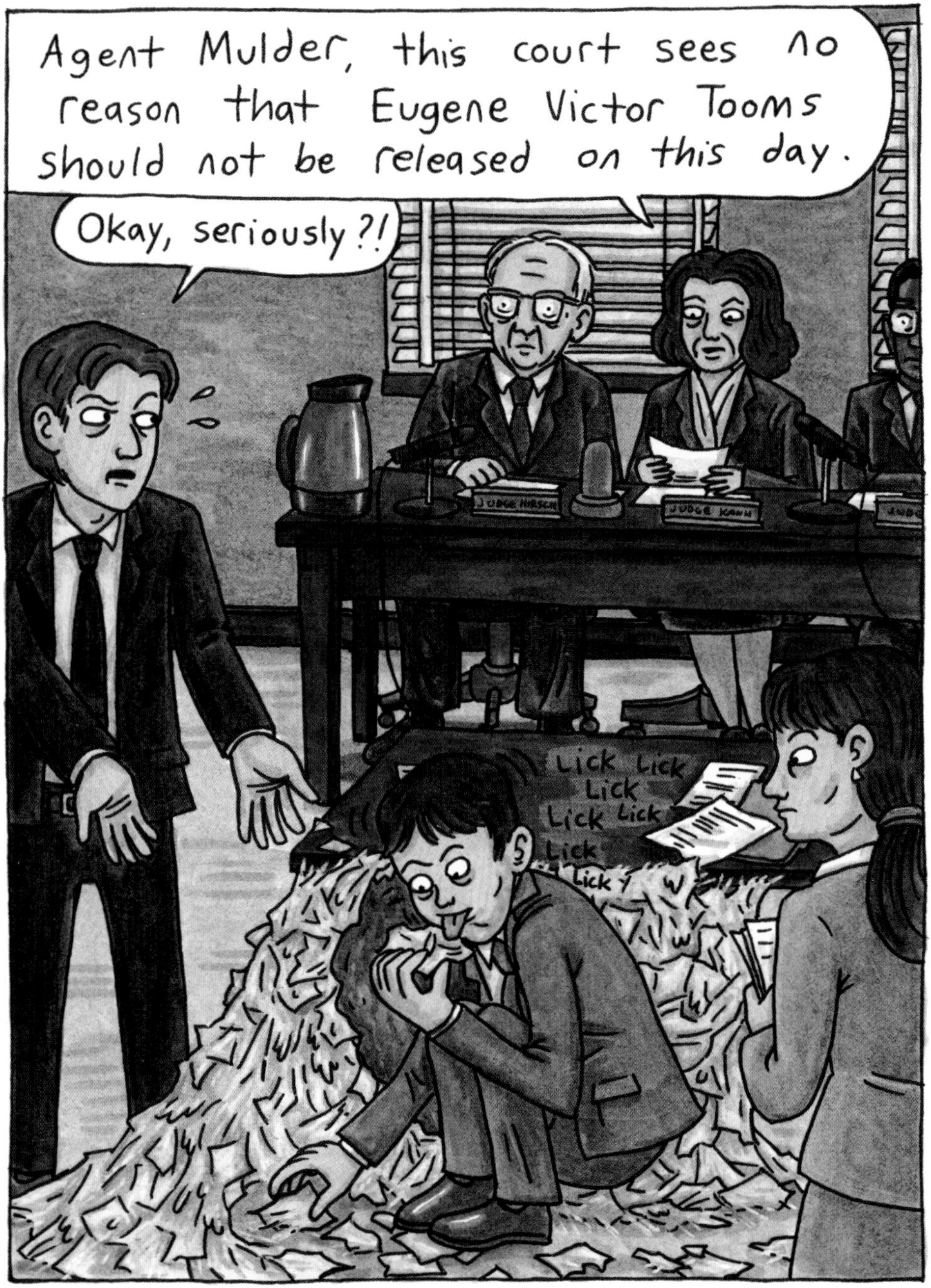
Agent Mulder, this court sees no reason that Eugene Victor Tooms should not be released on this day.
Okay, seriously?!
Lick Lick
Lick
Lick Lick
Lick
Lick

TOOMS

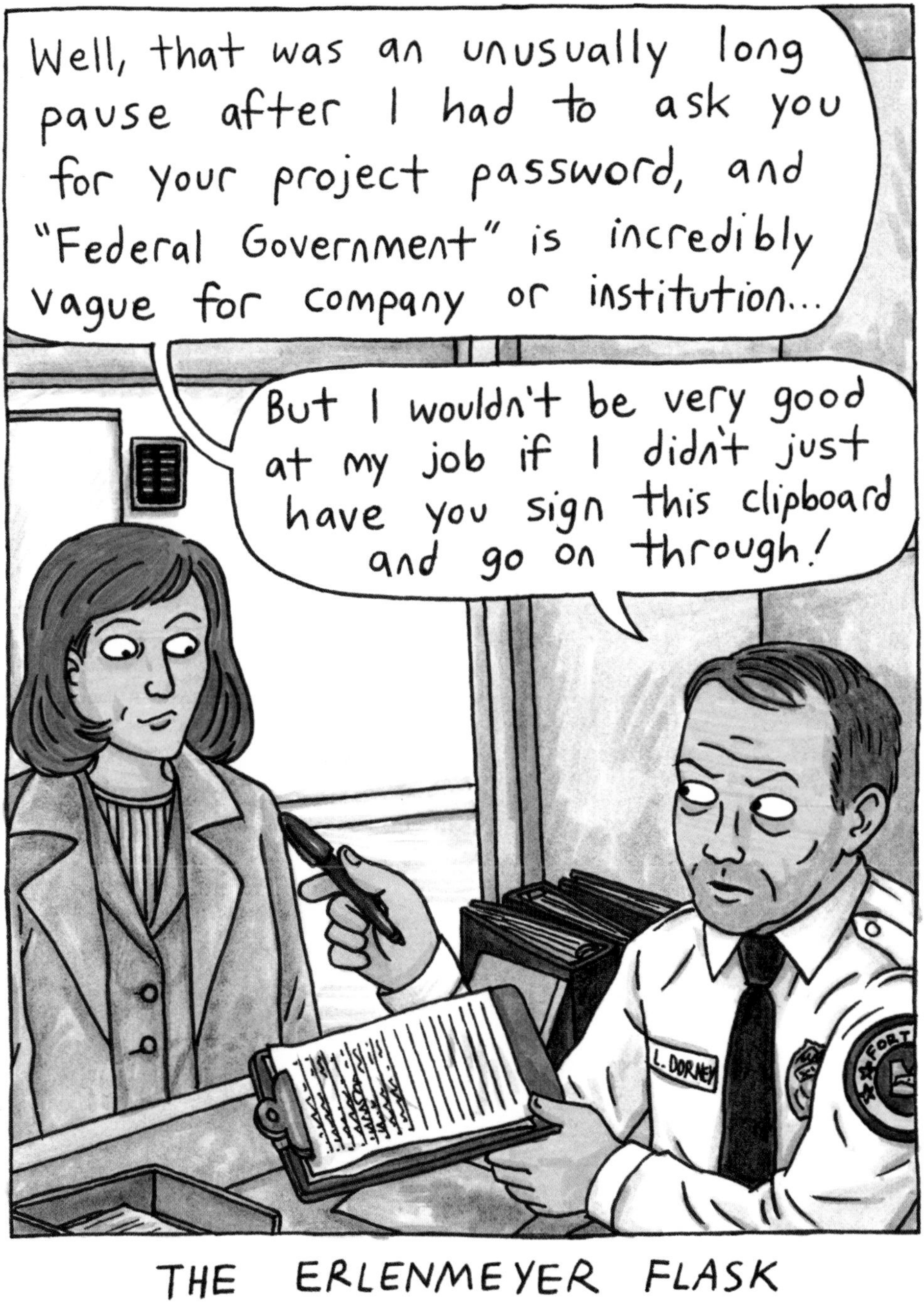

THE ERLENMEYER FLASK

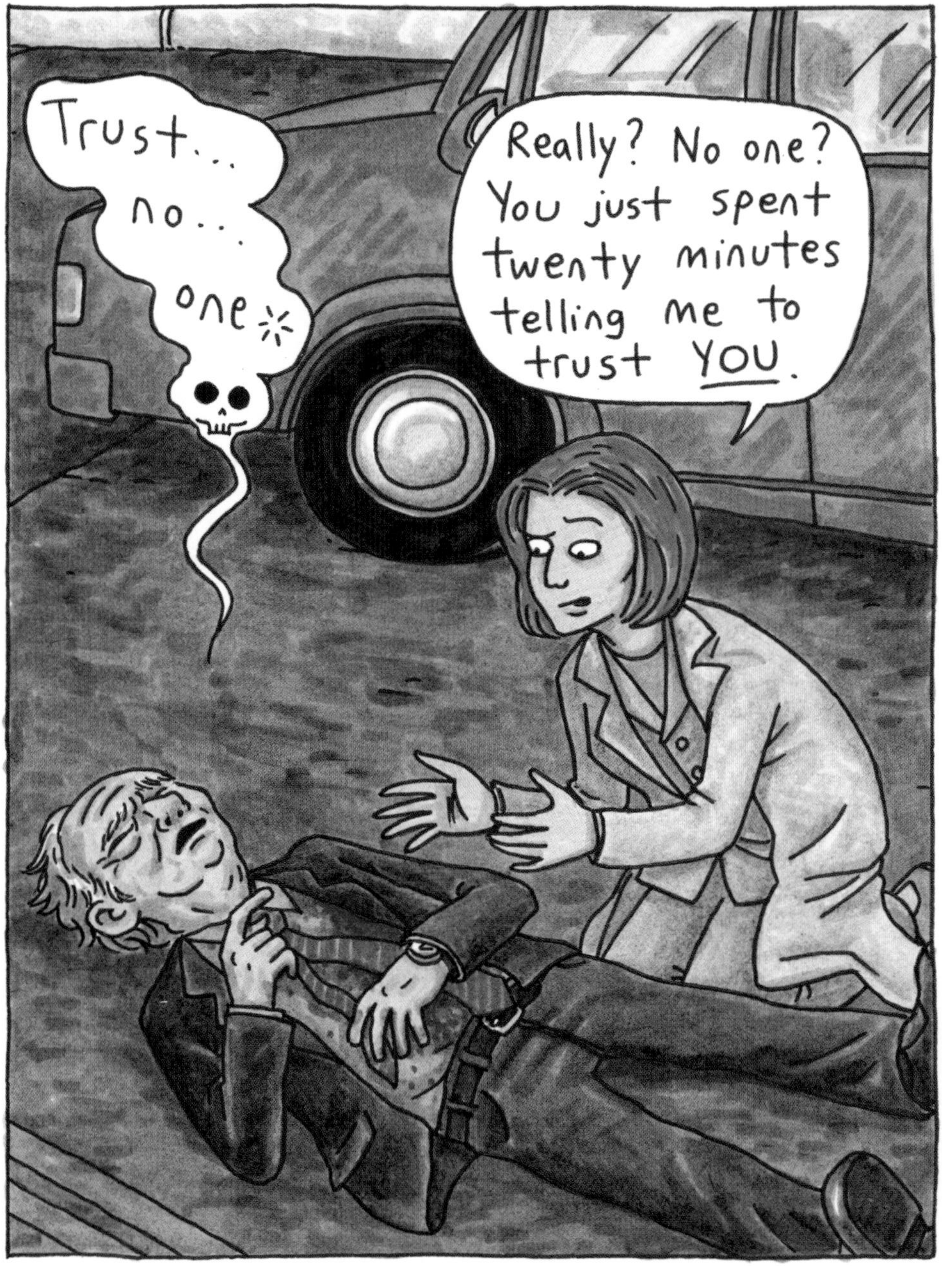
Trust... no... one
Really? No one? You just spent twenty minutes telling me to trust YOU.

TRUST NO ONE

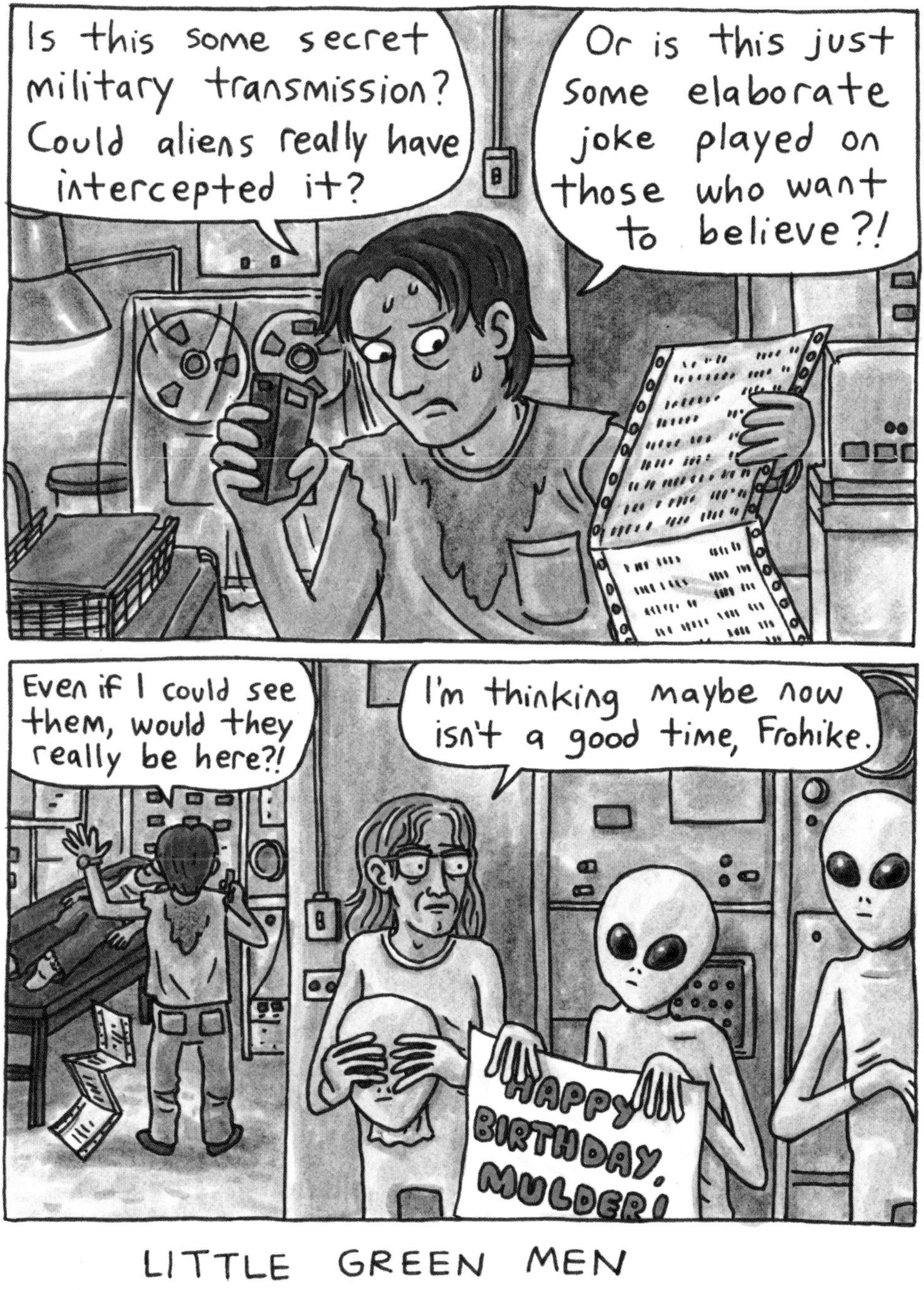
Is this some secret military transmission? Could aliens really have intercepted it?
Or is this just some elaborate joke played on those who want to believe?!
Even if I could see them, would they really be here?!
I'm thinking maybe now isn't a good time, Frohike.
HAPPY BIRTHDAY, MULDER!

LITTLE GREEN MEN

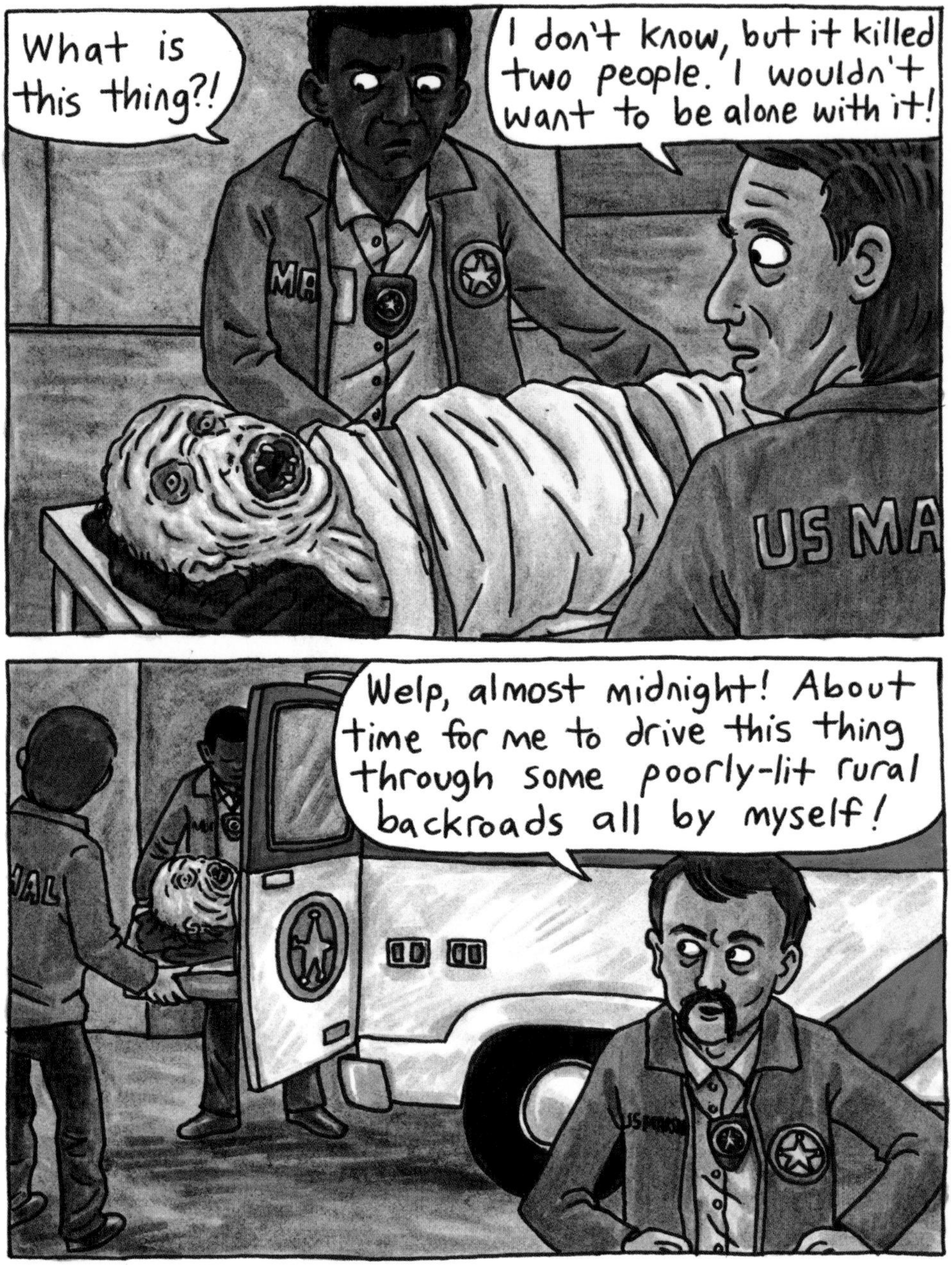
What is this thing?!
I don't know, but it killed two people. I wouldn't want to be alone with it!
US MA
Welp, almost midnight! About time for me to drive this thing through some poorly-lit rural backroads all by myself!

THE HOST

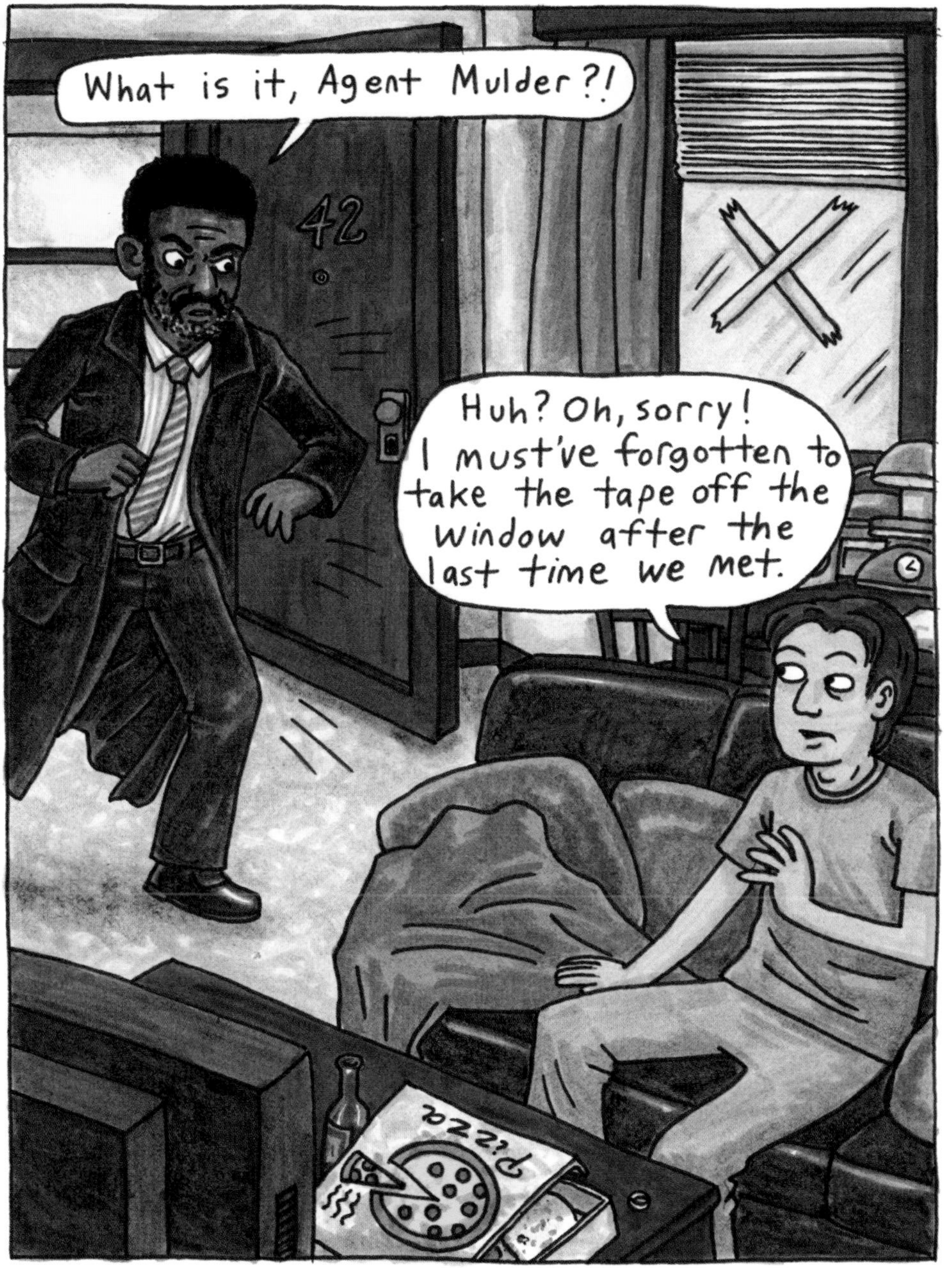
What is it, Agent Mulder?!
42
Huh? Oh, sorry! I must've forgotten to take the tape off the window after the last time we met.
Pizza

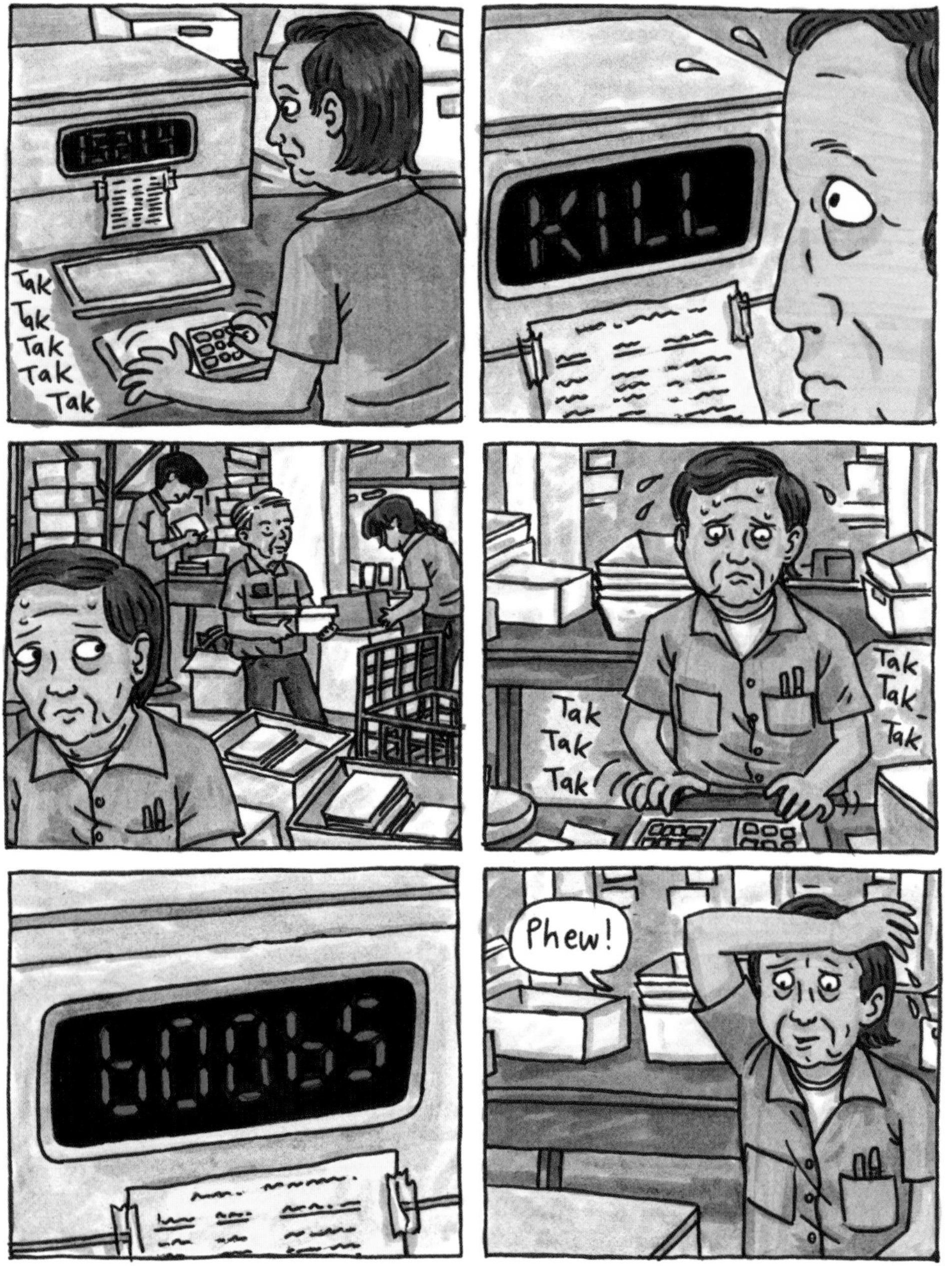
Tak
Tak
Tak
Tak
Tak
KILL
Tak
Tak
Tak
Tak
Tak
Tak
bOObS
Phew!

BLOOD

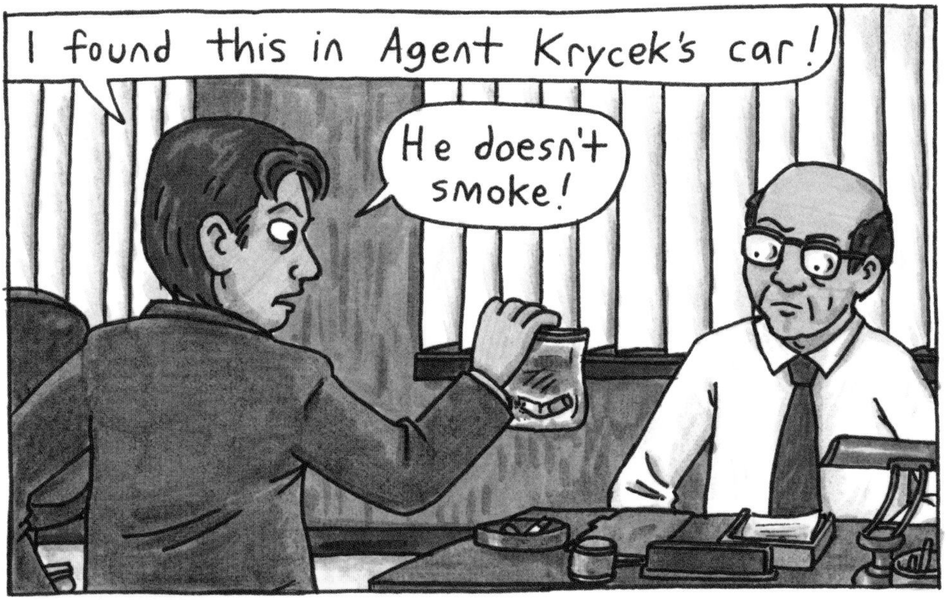
I found this in Agent Krycek's car!
He doesn't smoke!

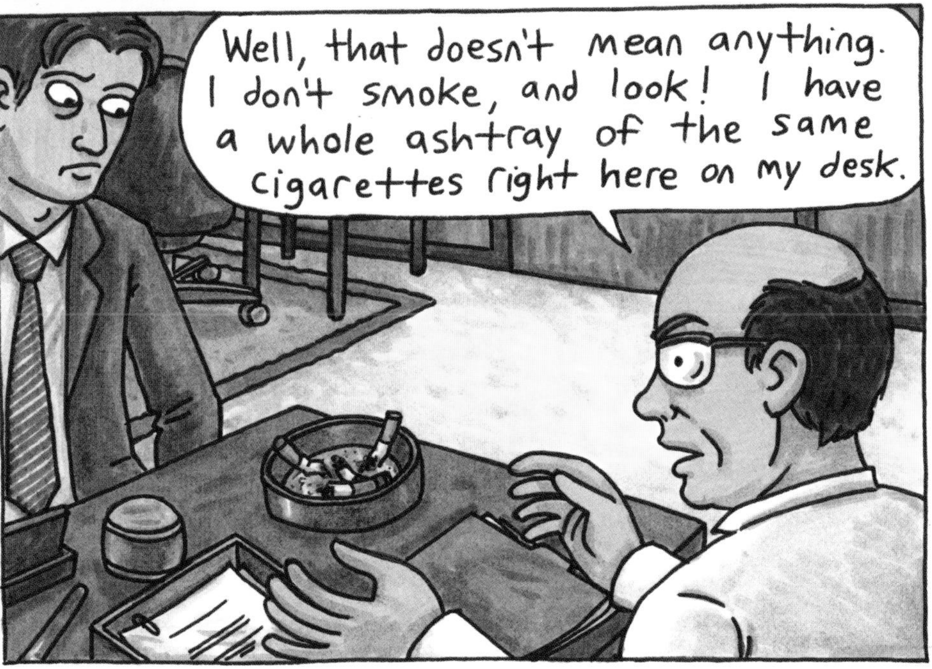
Well, that doesn't mean anything. I don't smoke, and look! I have a whole ashtray of the same cigarettes right here on my desk.

ASCENSION

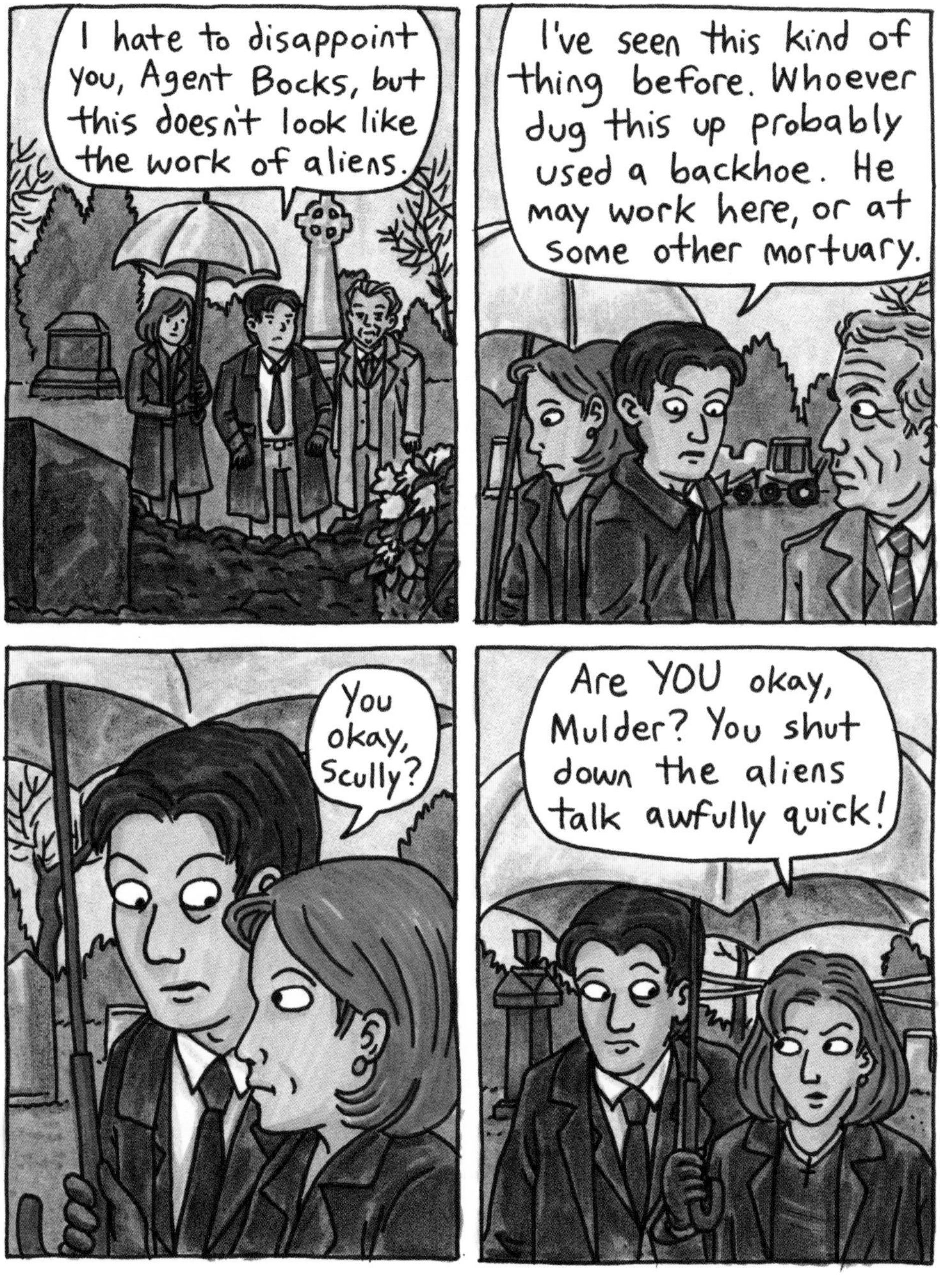
I hate to disappoint you, Agent Bocks, but this doesn't look like the work of aliens.
I've seen this kind of thing before. Whoever dug this up probably used a backhoe. He may work here, or at some other mortuary.
You okay, Scully?
Are YOU okay, Mulder? You shut down the aliens talk awfully quick!

IRRESISTIBLE

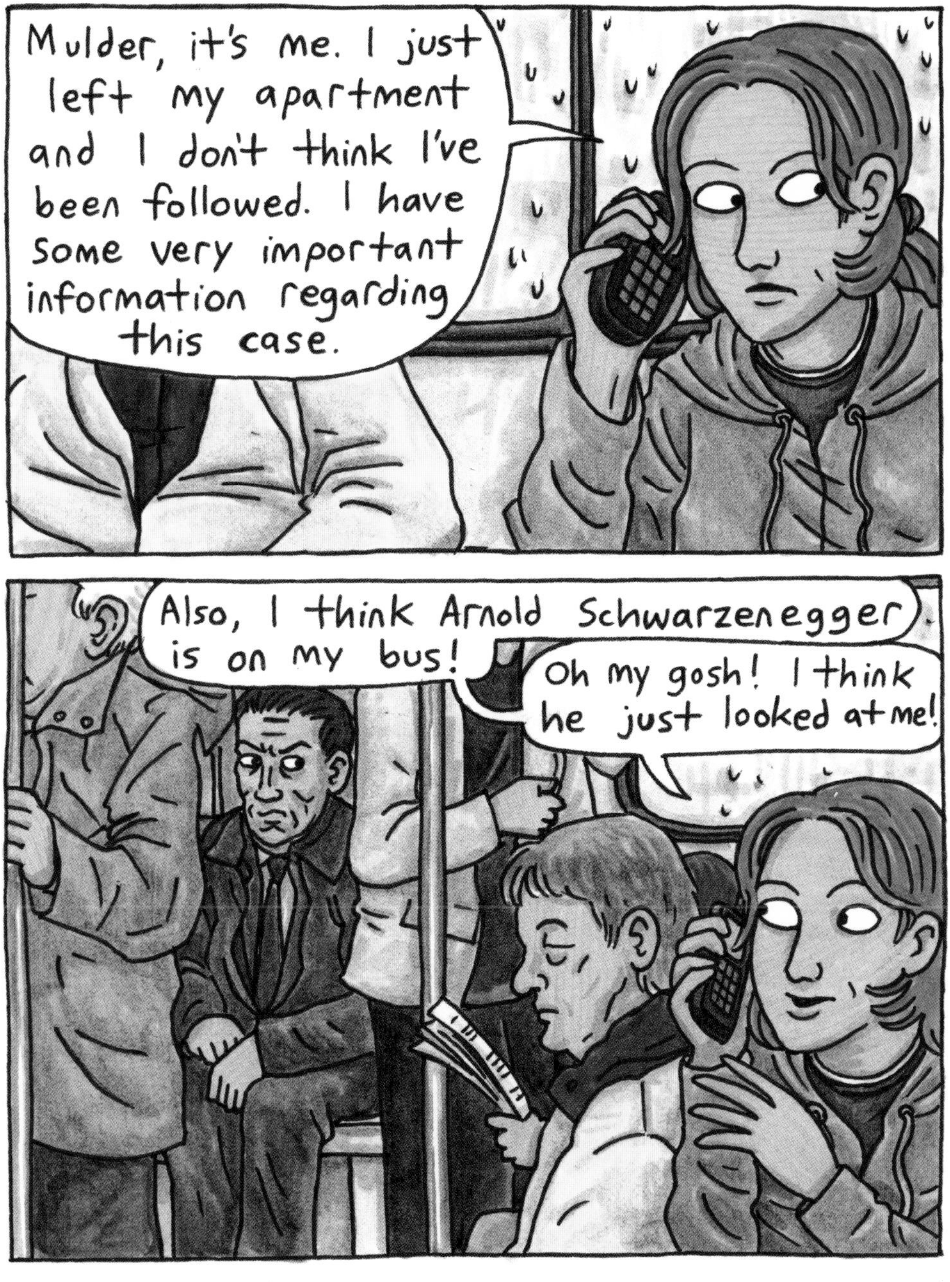
Mulder, it's me. I just left my apartment and I don't think I've been followed. I have some very important information regarding this case.
Also, I think Arnold Schwarzenegger is on my bus!
Oh my gosh! I think he just looked at me!

COLONY

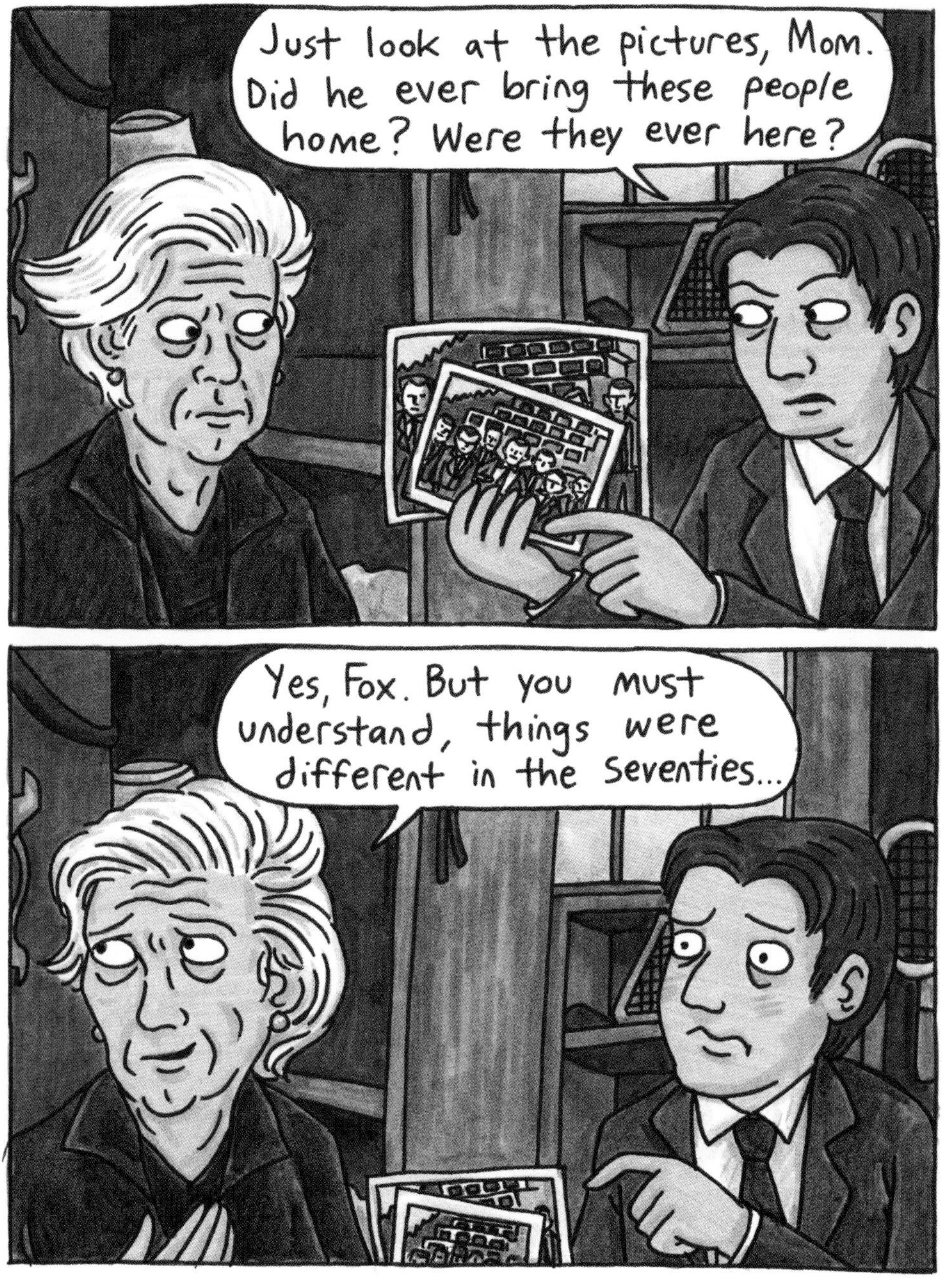
Just look at the pictures, Mom. Did he ever bring these people home? Were they ever here?
Yes, Fox. But you must understand, things were different in the seventies...

THE BLESSING WAY

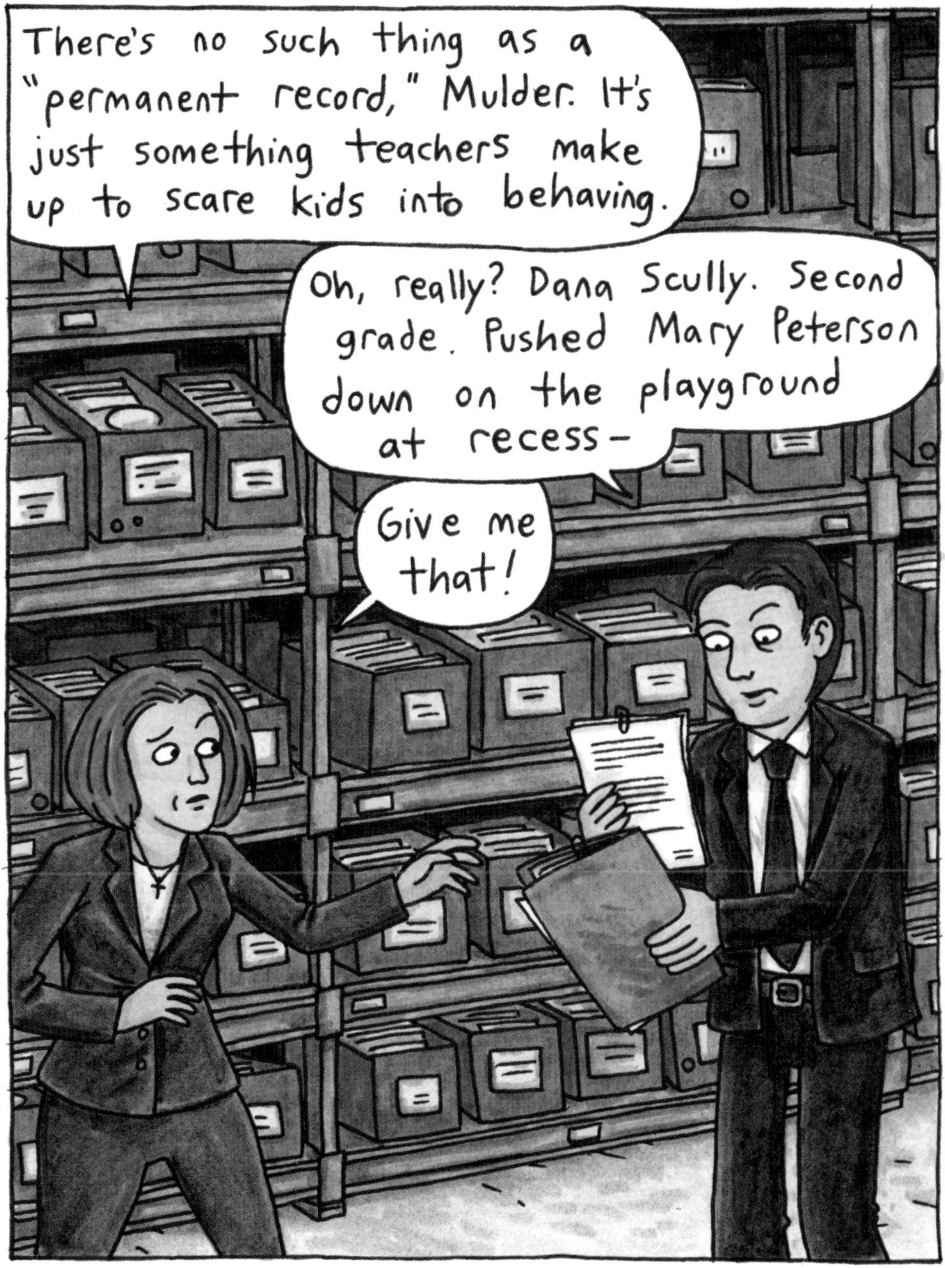
There's no such thing as a "permanent record," Mulder. It's just something teachers make up to scare kids into behaving.
Oh, really? Dana Scully. Second grade. Pushed Mary Peterson down on the playground at recess-
Give me that!

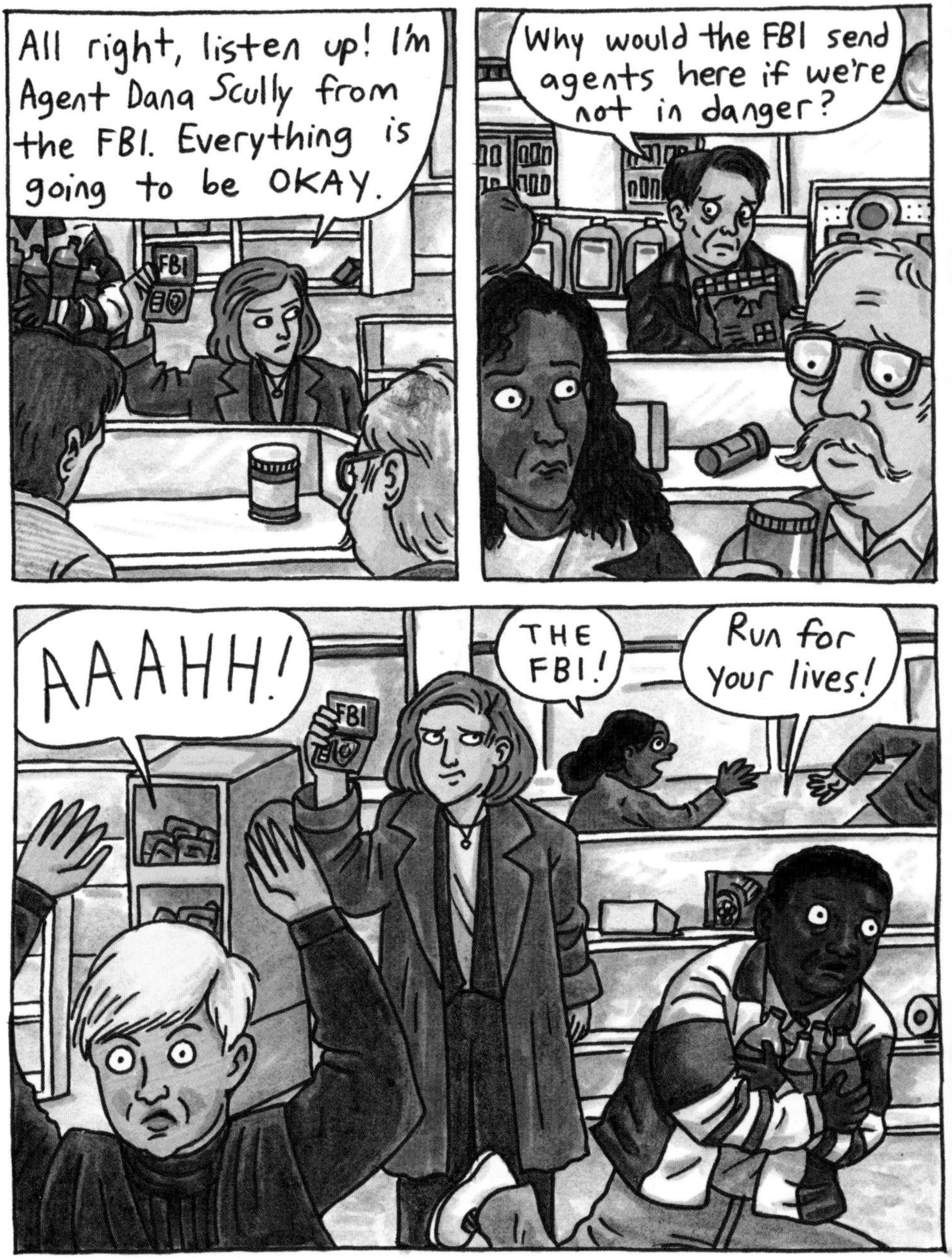
All right, listen up! I'm Agent Dana Scully from the FBI. Everything is going to be OKAY.
FBI
Why would the FBI send agents here if we're not in danger?
AAAHH!
FBI
THE FBI!
Run for your lives!

WAR OF THE COPROPHAGES

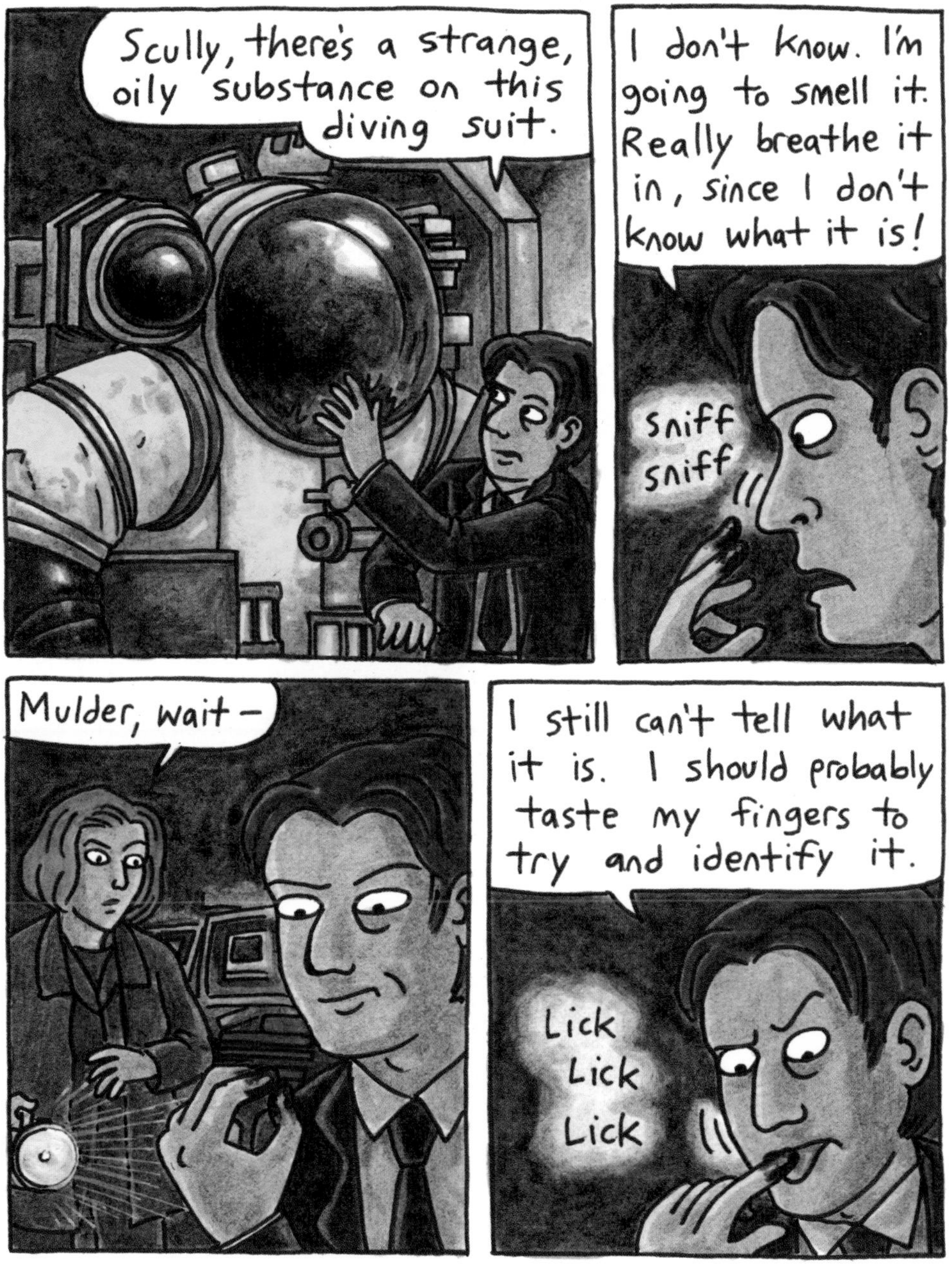
Scully, there's a strange, oily substance on this diving suit.
I don't know. I'm going to smell it. Really breathe it in, since I don't know what it is!
sniff sniff
Mulder, wait—
I still can't tell what it is. I should probably taste my fingers to try and identify it.
Lick Lick Lick

PIPER MARU

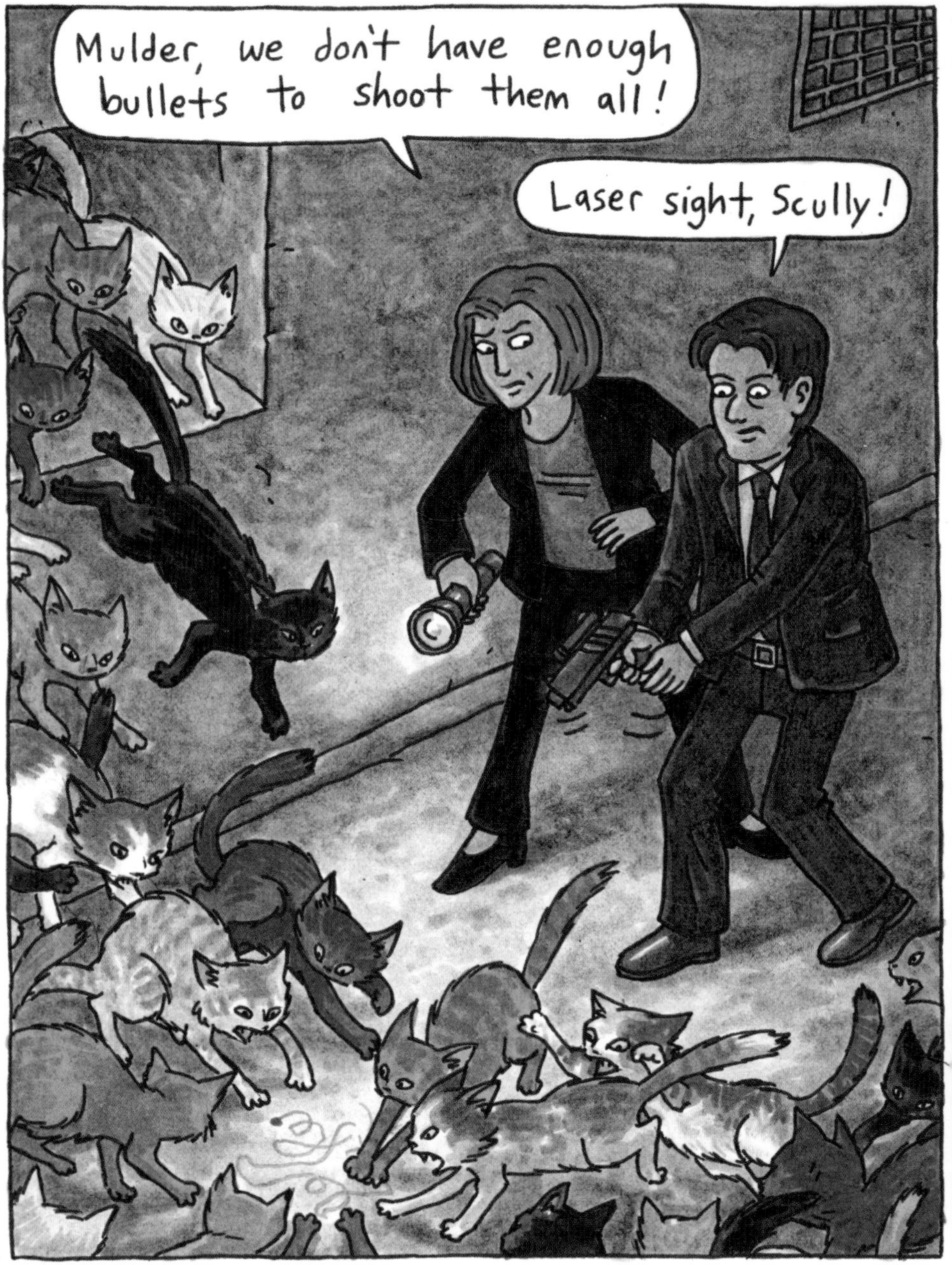
Mulder, we don't have enough bullets to shoot them all!
Laser sight, Scully!

TESO DOS BICHOS

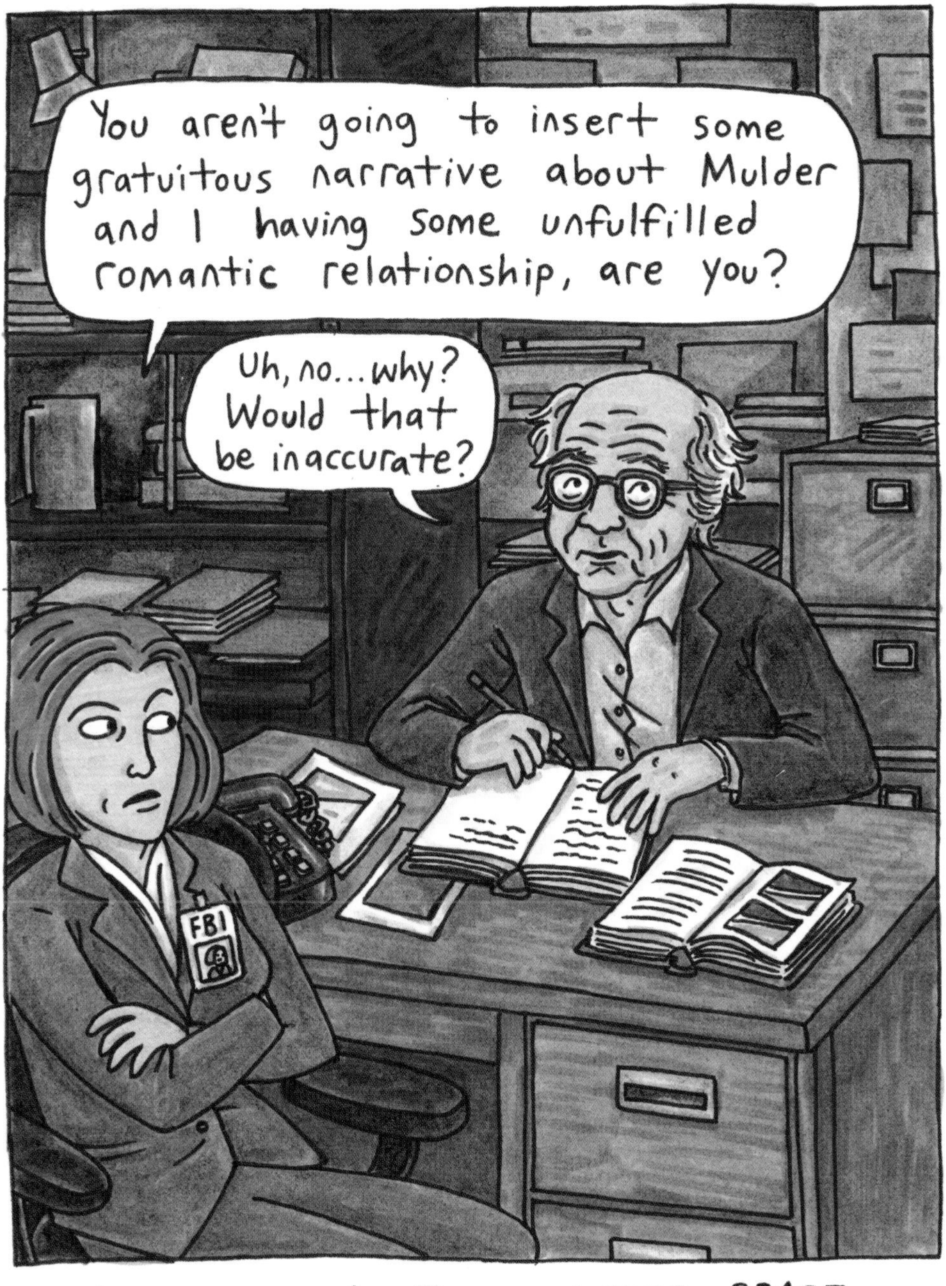
You aren't going to insert some gratuitous narrative about Mulder and I having some unfulfilled romantic relationship, are you?
Uh, no... why? Would that be inaccurate?
FBI

JOSE CHUNG'S FROM OUTER SPACE

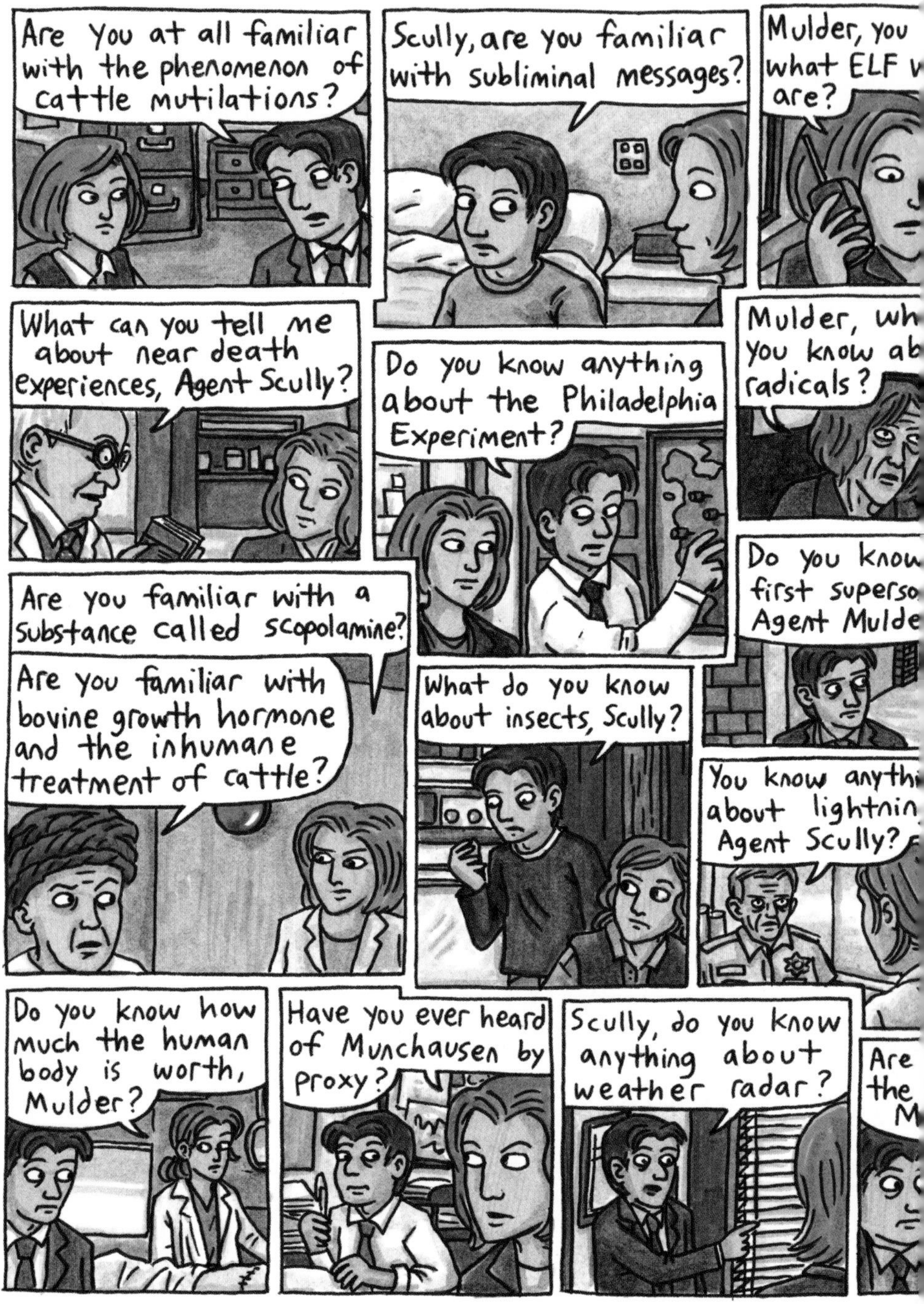
Are you at all familiar with the phenomenon of cattle mutilations?
Scully, are you familiar with subliminal messages?
Mulder, you what ELF are?
What can you tell me about near death experiences, Agent Scully?
Do you know anything about the Philadelphia Experiment?
Mulder, wh you know ab radicals?
Do you know first superso Agent Mulde
Are you familiar with a substance called scopolamine?
Are you familiar with bovine growth hormone and the inhumane treatment of cattle?
What do you know about insects, Scully?
You know anythi about lightnin Agent Scully?
Do you know how much the human body is worth, Mulder?
Have you ever heard of Munchausen by proxy?
Scully, do you know anything about weather radar?
Are the M

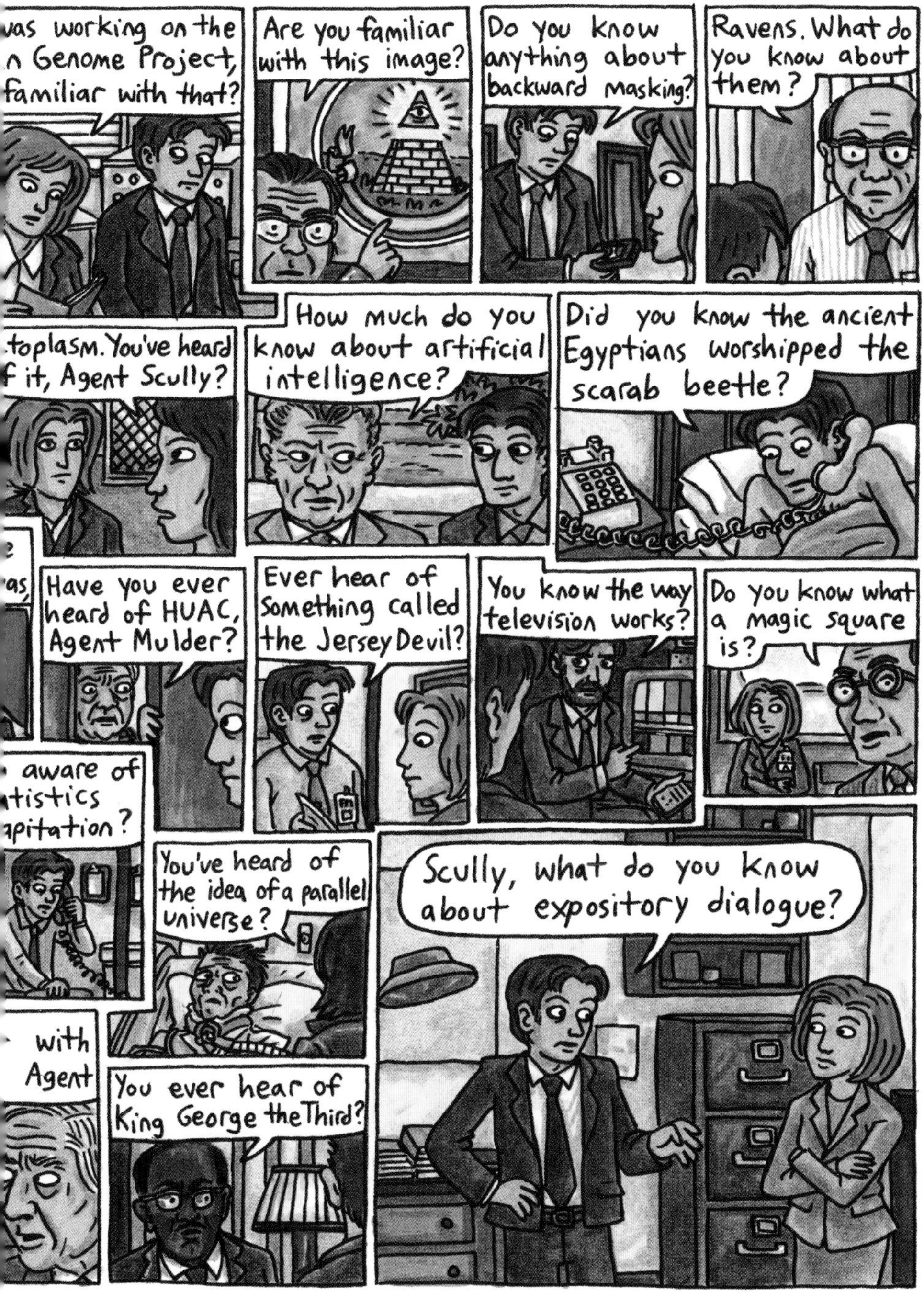
vas working on the n Genome Project, familiar with that?
Are you familiar with this image?
Do you know anything about backward masking?
Ravens. What do you know about them?
toplasm. You've heard f it, Agent Scully?
How much do you know about artificial intelligence?
Did you know the ancient Egyptians worshipped the scarab beetle?
Have you ever heard of HUAC, Agent Mulder?
Ever hear of something called the Jersey Devil?
You know the way television works?
Do you know what a magic square is?
aware of tistics apitation?
You've heard of the idea of a parallel universe?
with Agent
You ever hear of King George the Third?
Scully, what do you know about expository dialogue?

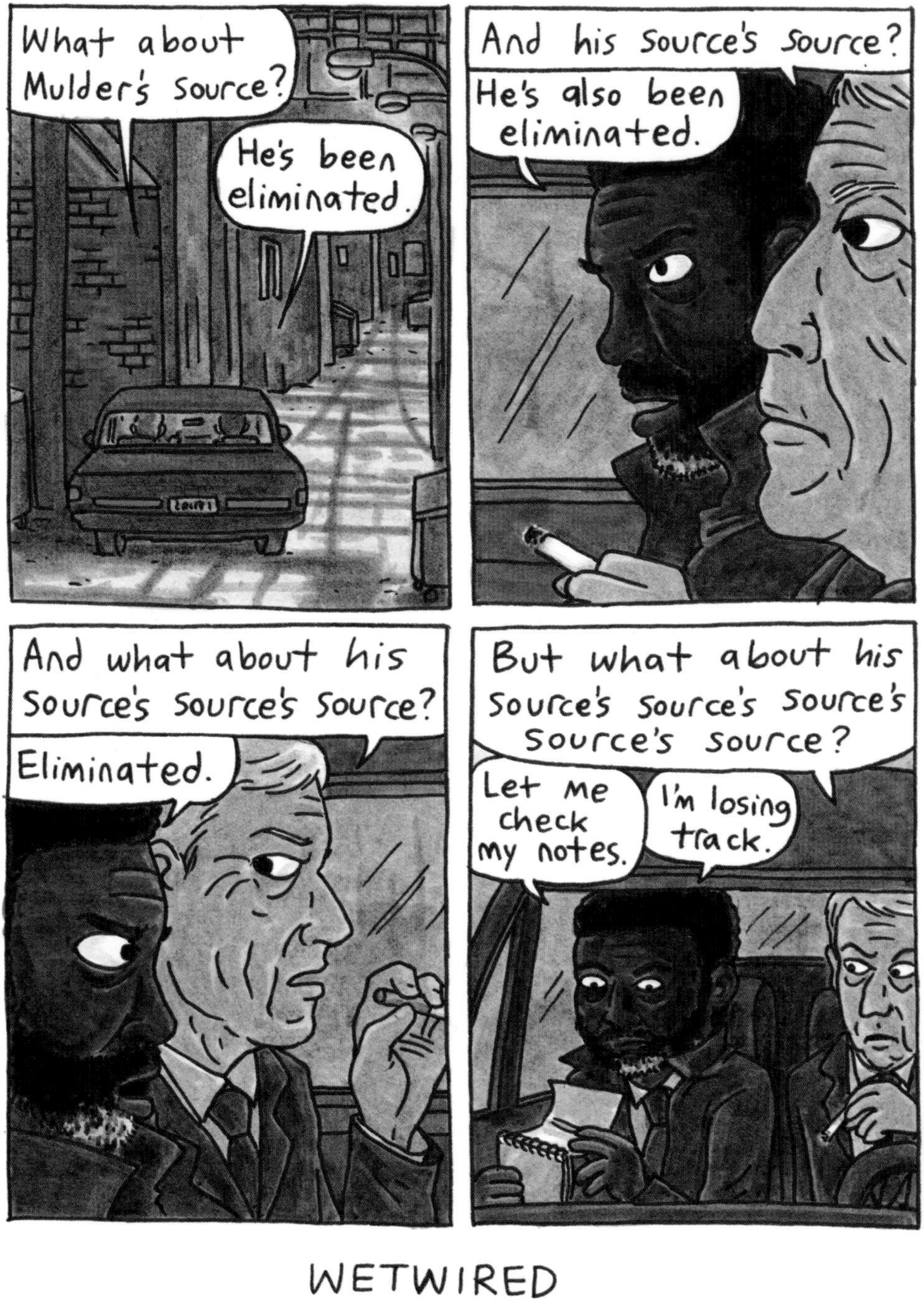
What about Mulder's source?
He's been eliminated.
And his source's source?
He's also been eliminated.
And what about his source's source's source?
Eliminated.
But what about his source's source's source's source's source?
Let me check my notes.
I'm losing track.

WETWIRED

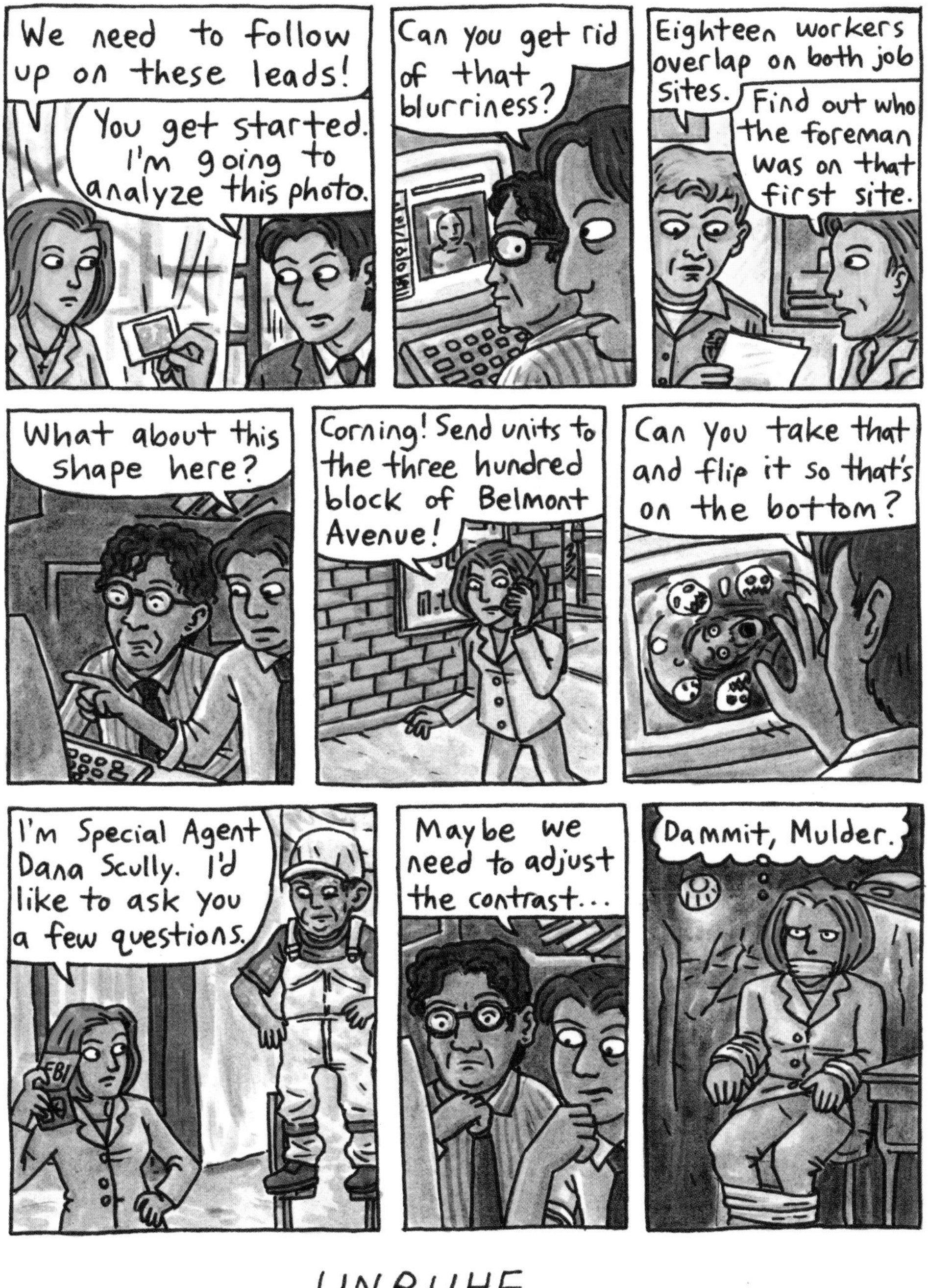
We need to follow up on these leads!
You get started. I'm going to analyze this photo.
Can you get rid of that blurriness?
Eighteen workers overlap on both job sites.
Find out who the foreman was on that first site.
What about this shape here?
Corning! Send units to the three hundred block of Belmont Avenue!
Can you take that and flip it so that's on the bottom?
I'm Special Agent Dana Scully. I'd like to ask you a few questions.
FBI
Maybe we need to adjust the contrast...
Dammit, Mulder.

UNRUHE

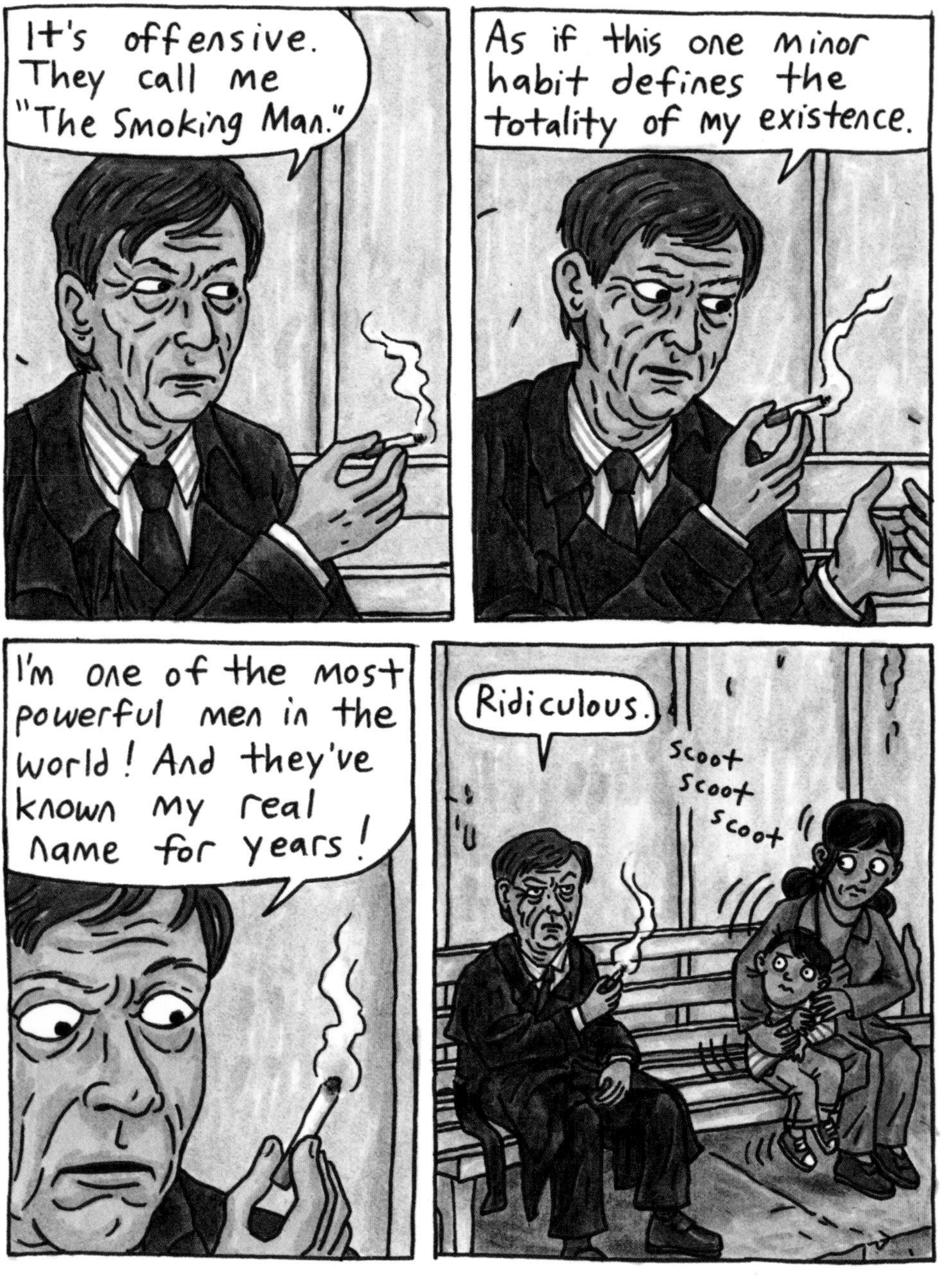
It's offensive. They call me "The Smoking Man."
As if this one minor habit defines the totality of my existence.
I'm one of the most powerful men in the world! And they've known my real name for years!
Ridiculous.
Scoot
Scoot
Scoot

MUSINGS OF A CIGARETTE SMOKING MAN

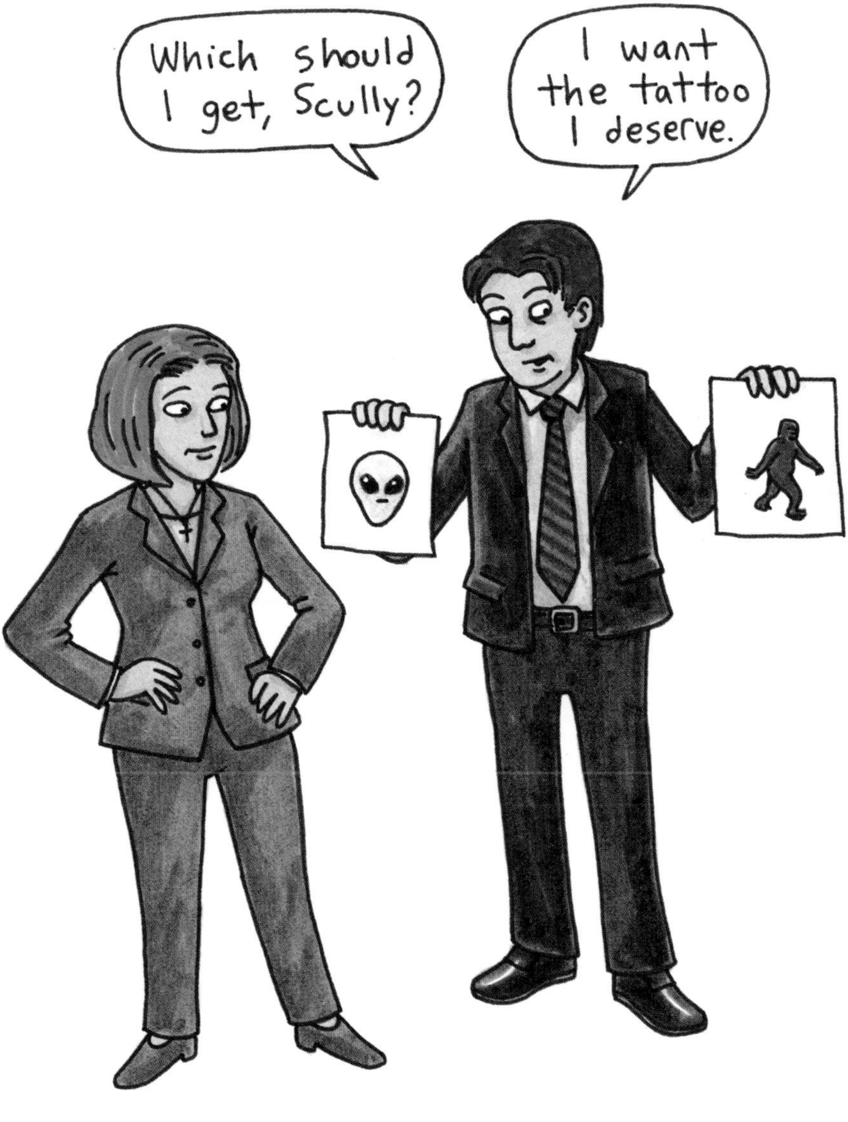
Which should I get, Scully?
I want the tattoo I deserve.

NEVER AGAIN

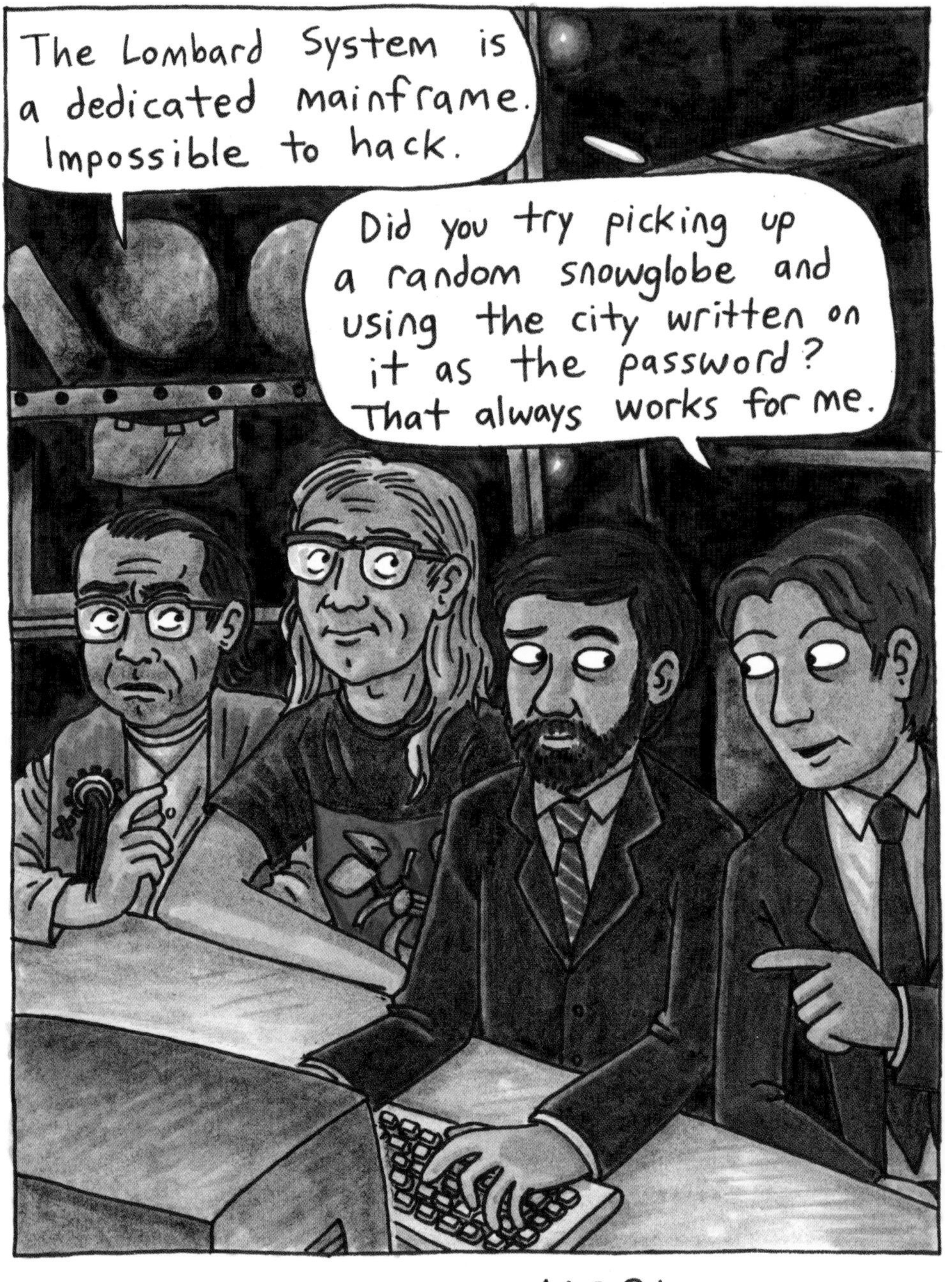
The Lombard System is a dedicated mainframe. Impossible to hack.
Did you try picking up a random snowglobe and using the city written on it as the password? That always works for me.

MEMENTO MORI

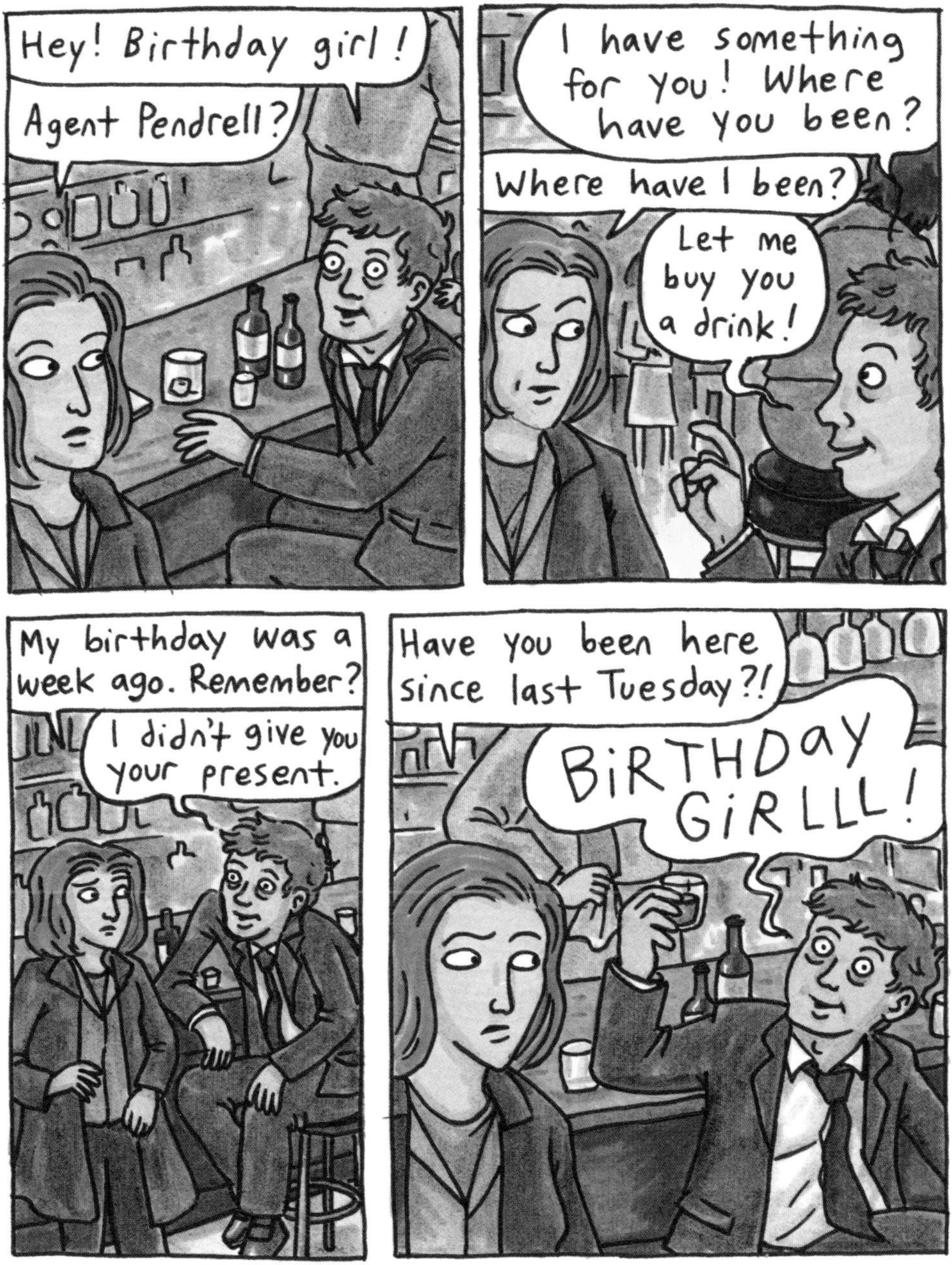
Hey! Birthday girl!
Agent Pendrell?
I have something for you! Where have you been?
Where have I been?
Let me buy you a drink!
My birthday was a week ago. Remember?
I didn't give you your present.
Have you been here since last Tuesday?!
BiRTHDay GiRLLL!

TEMPUS FUGIT

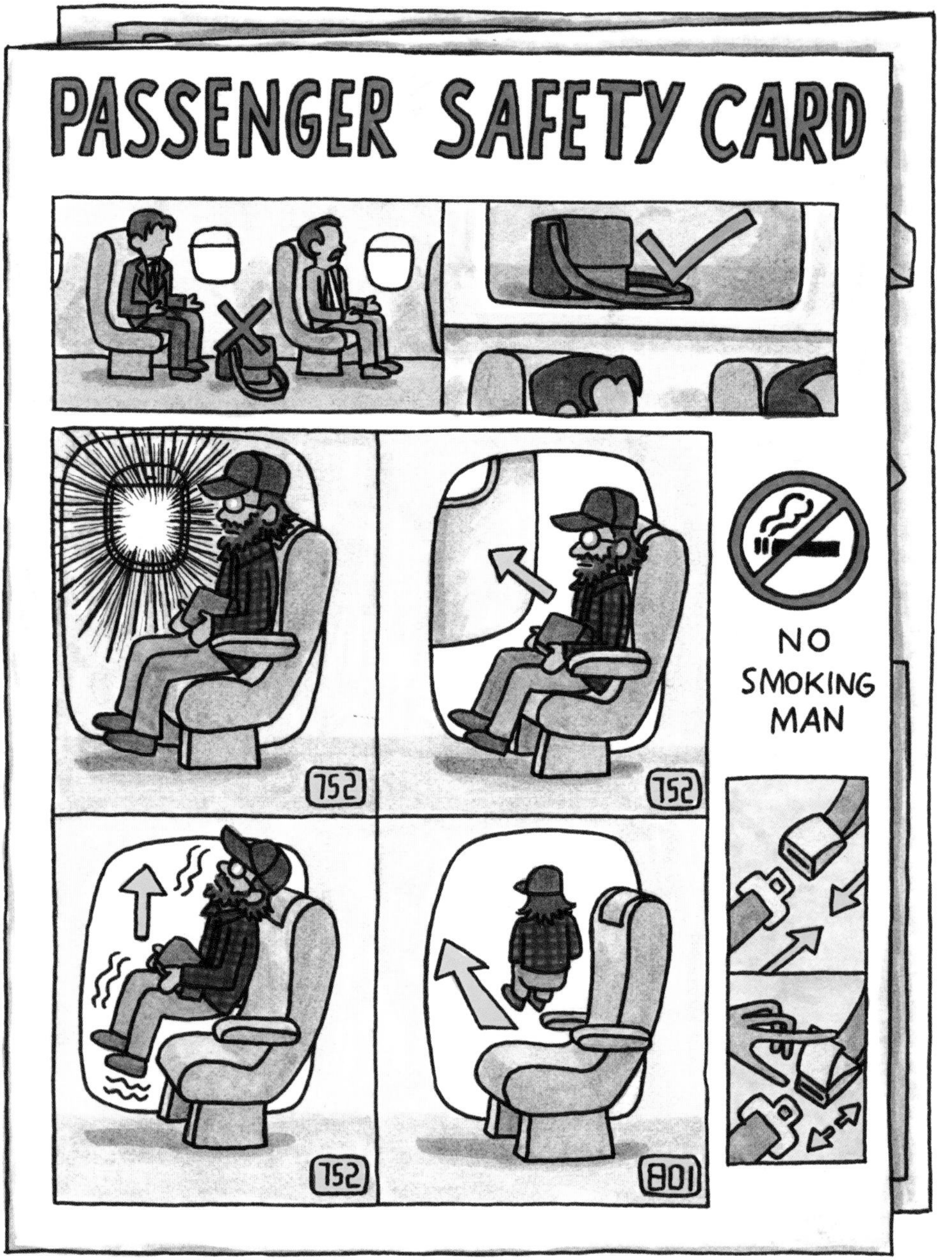
PASSENGER SAFETY CARD
752
752
NO
SMOKING
MAN
752
801

MAX

Derma is hairless. Grey with a foamy, latex texture.

There are four rubbery digits on each hand and three on each foot.

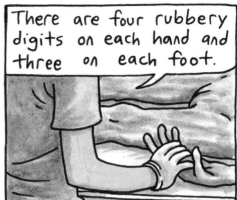

The eyes are lidless, glassy black, and covered by a thin membrane, attached by a glue-like substance.

The rib cage has the density of a relatively hard plastic, with a synthetic odor.

Examination of the chest cavity confirms what appears to be a collection of random hoses, tubes, and thin wires.

So, definitely not a movie prop!

GETHSEMANE

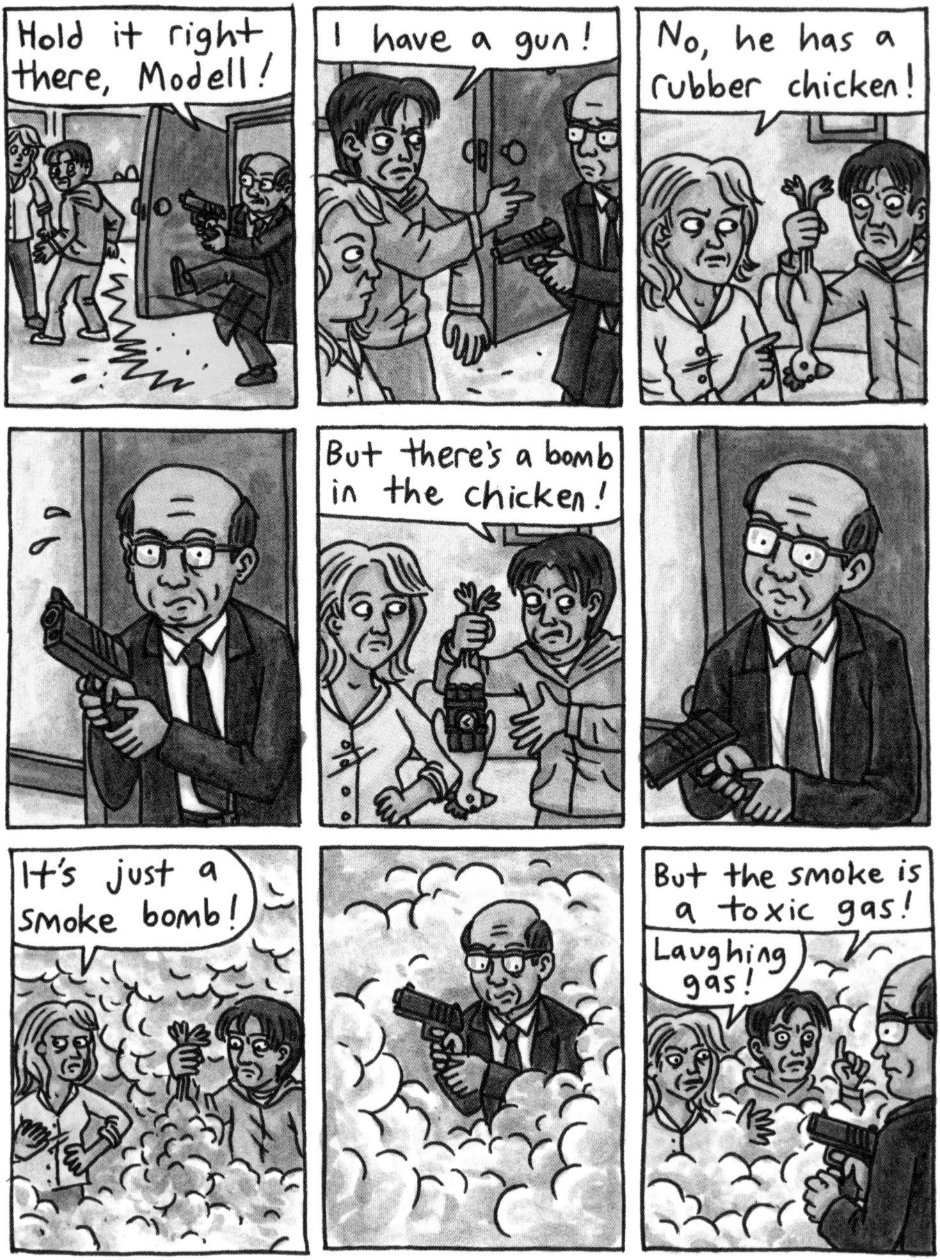
Hold it right there, Modell!
I have a gun!
No, he has a rubber chicken!
But there's a bomb in the chicken!
It's just a smoke bomb!
But the smoke is a toxic gas!
Laughing gas!

KITSUNEGARI

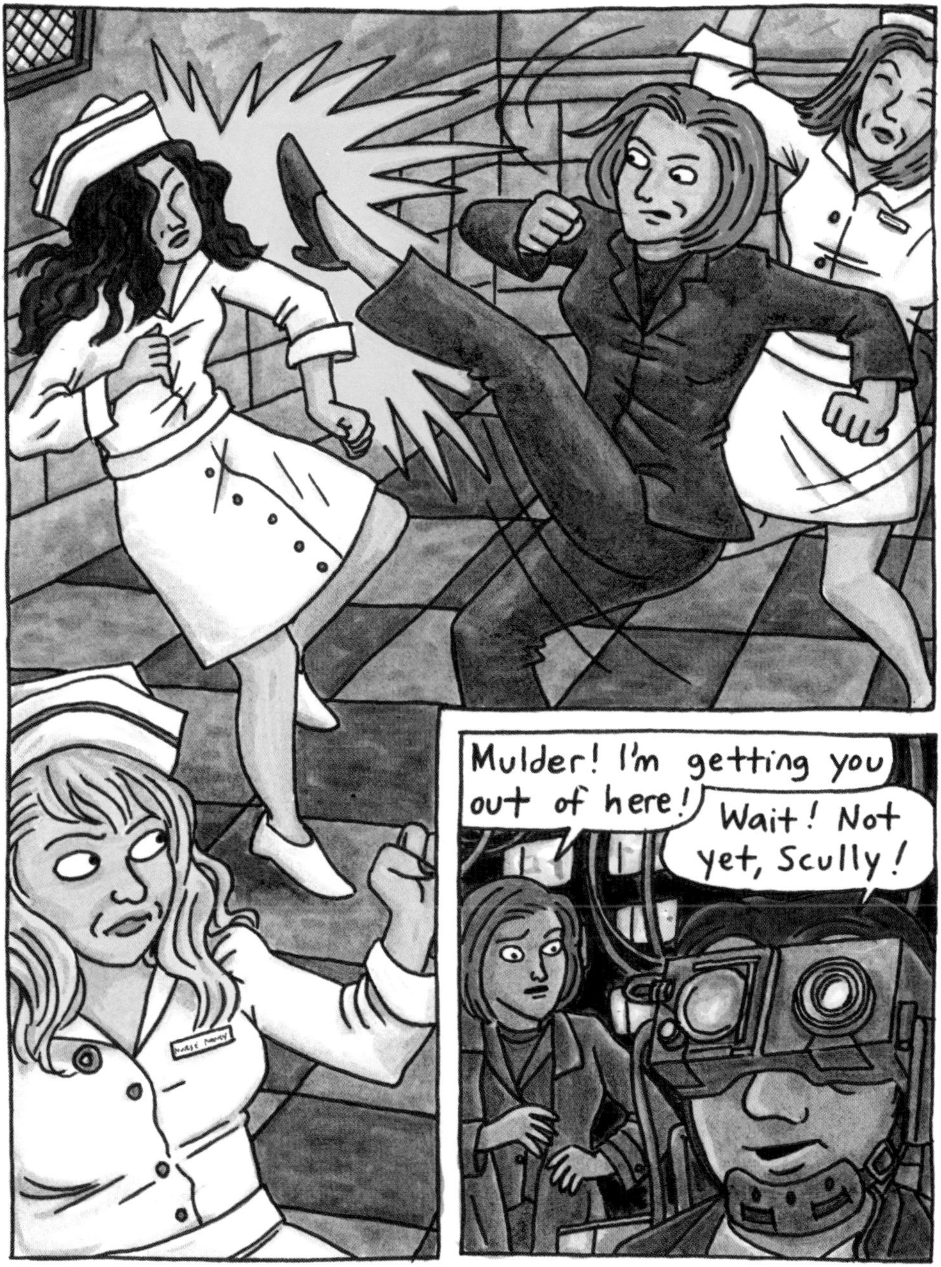
Mulder! I'm getting you out of here!
Wait! Not yet, Scully!

KILL SWITCH

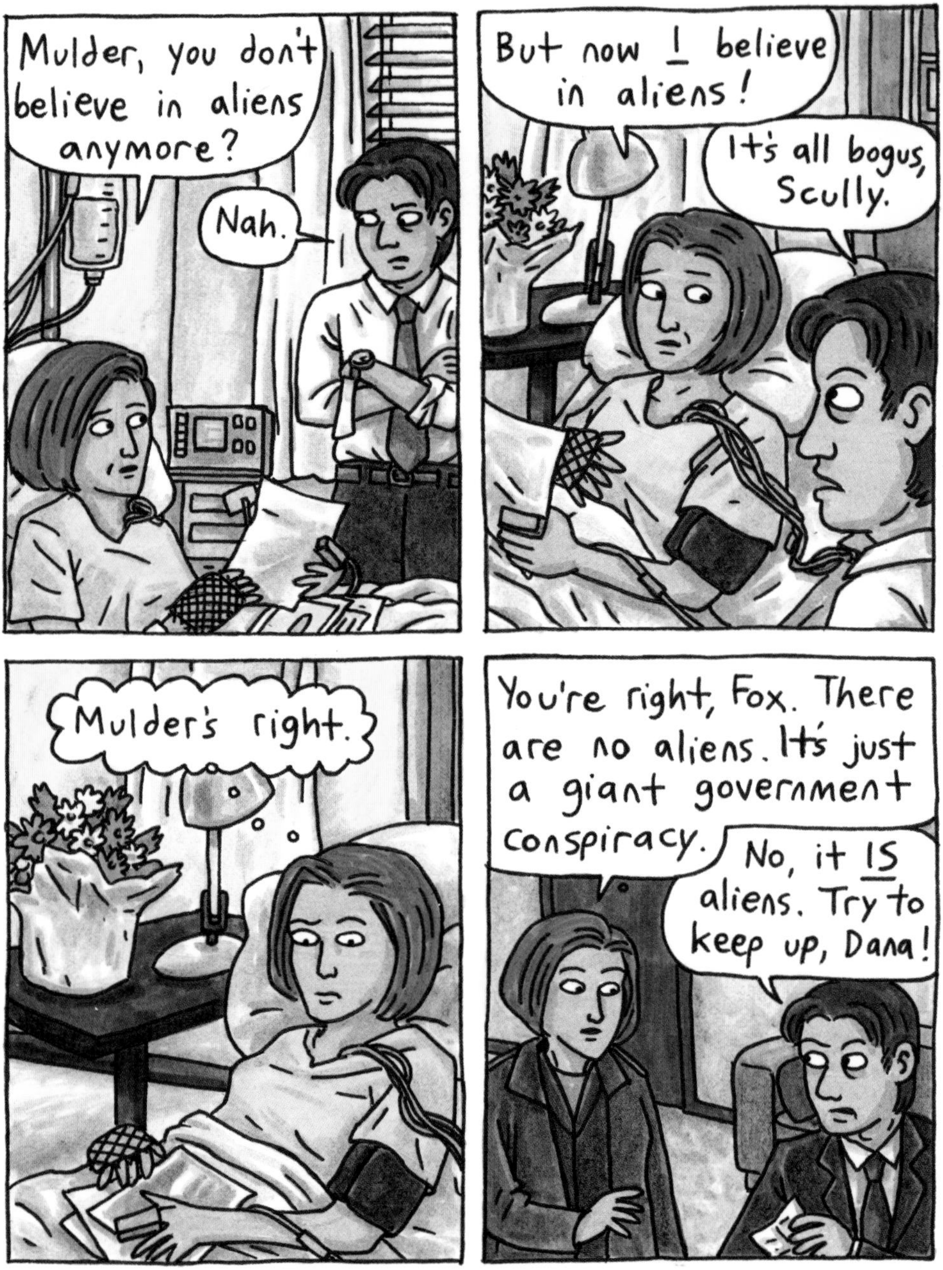
Mulder, you don't believe in aliens anymore?
Nah.
But now I believe in aliens!
It's all bogus, Scully.
Mulder's right.
You're right, Fox. There are no aliens. It's just a giant government conspiracy.
No, it IS aliens. Try to keep up, Dana!

THE RED AND THE BLACK

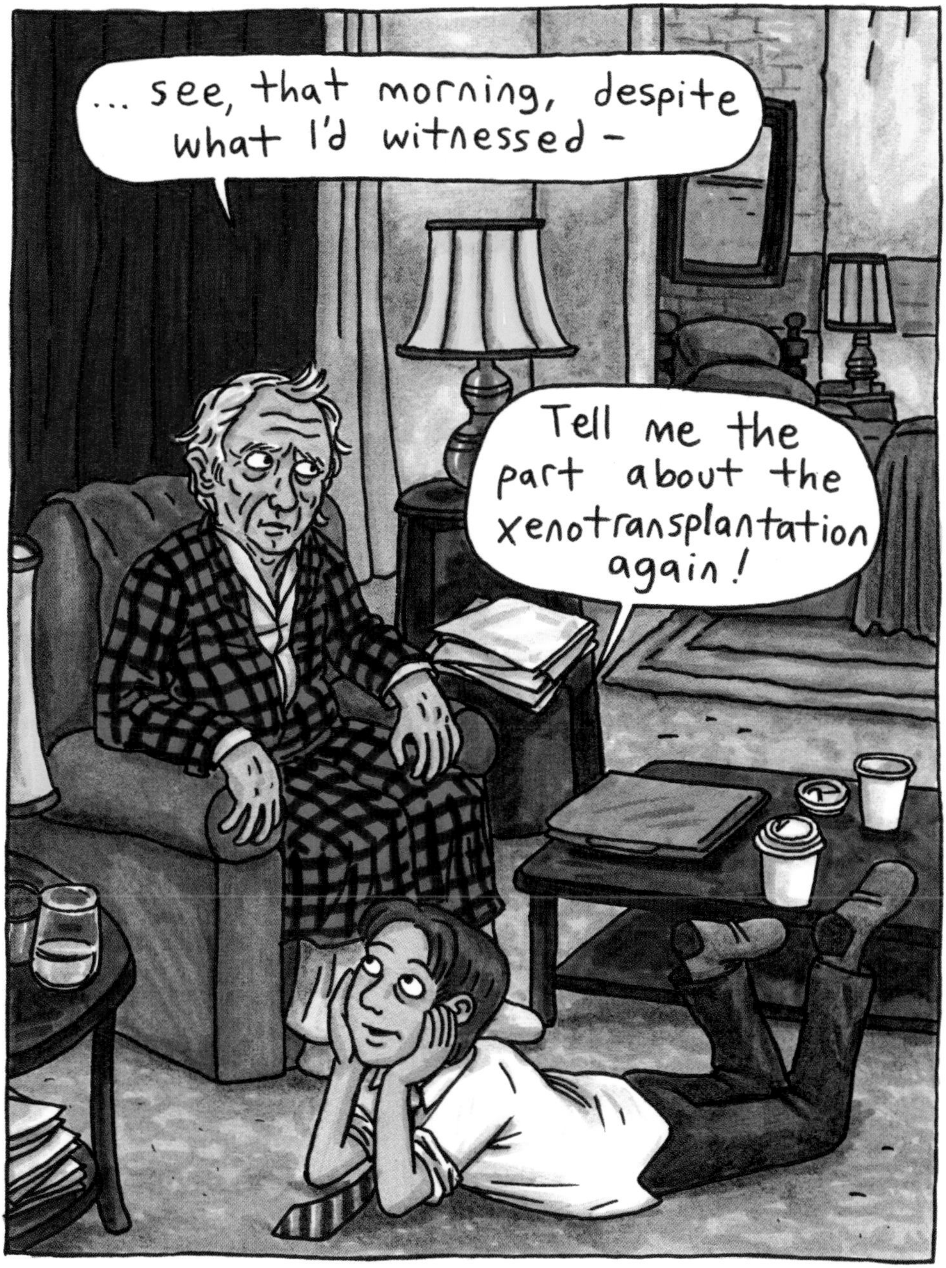
... see, that morning, despite what I'd witnessed -
Tell me the part about the xenotransplantation again!

TRAVELERS

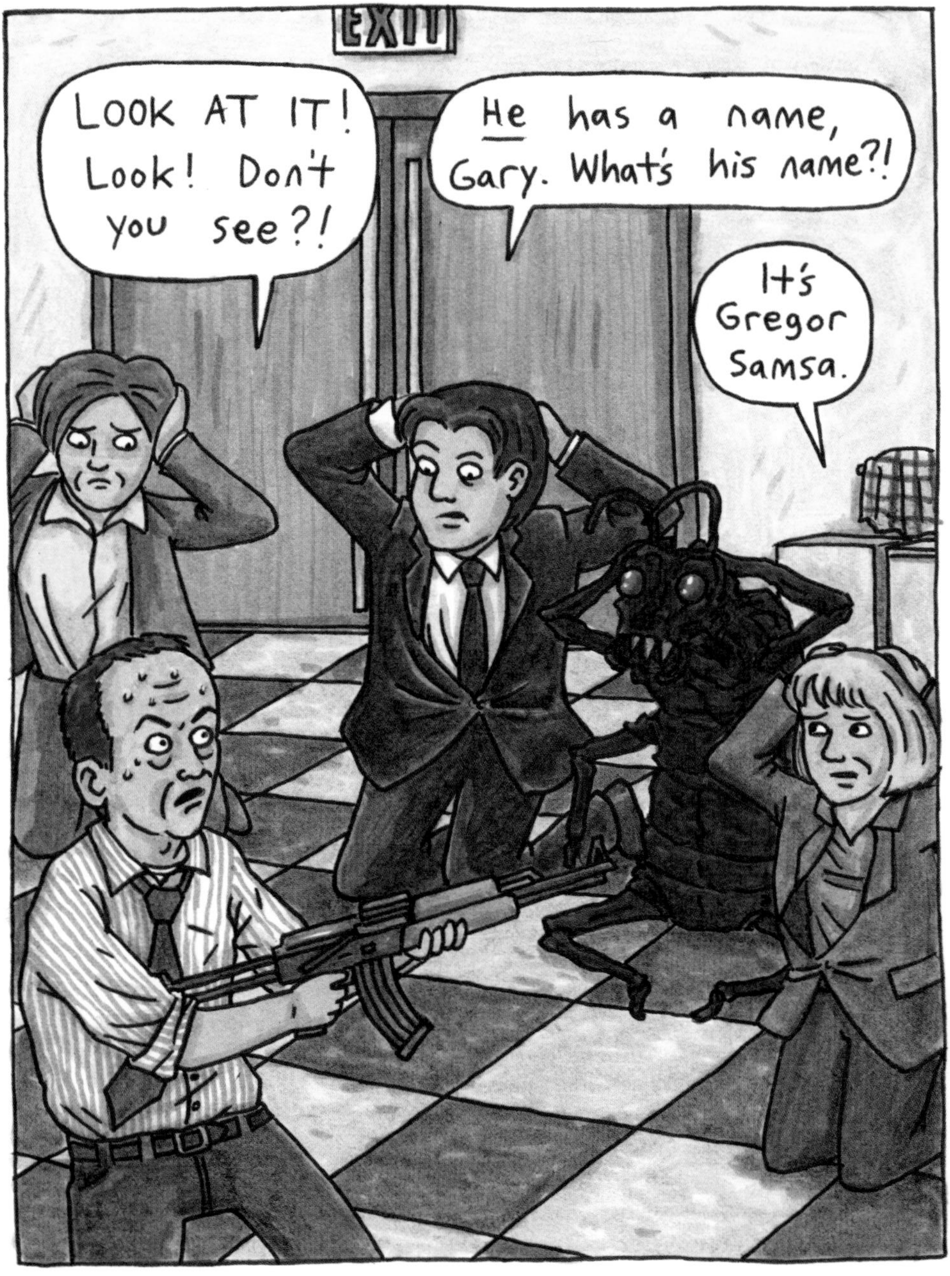
EXIT
LOOK AT IT! Look! Don't you see?!
He has a name, Gary. What's his name?!
It's Gregor Samsa.

FOLIE À DEUX

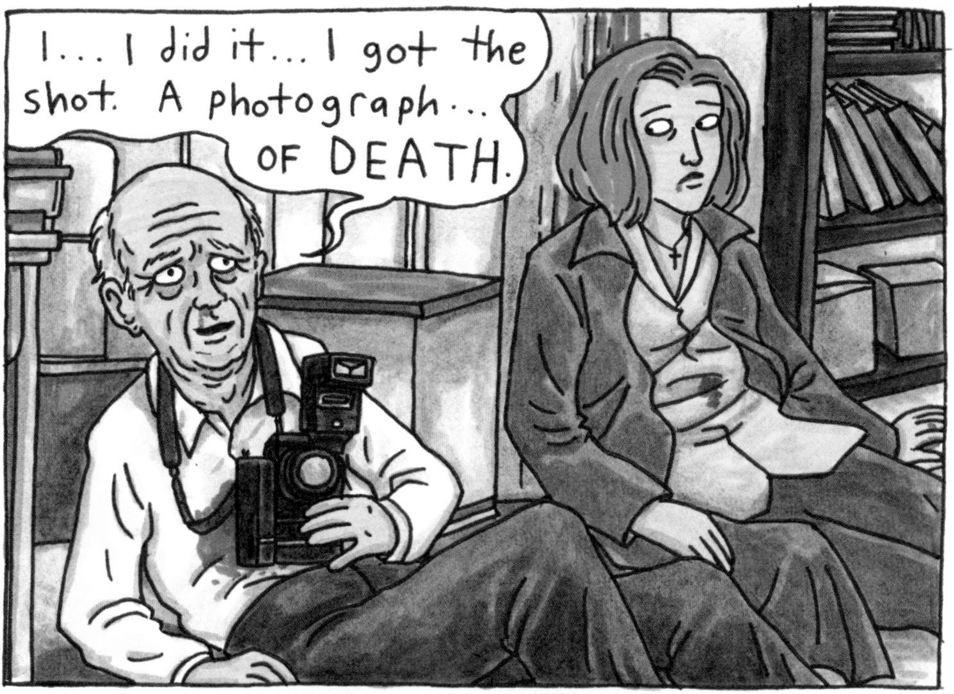
I... I did it... I got the shot. A photograph... OF DEATH.

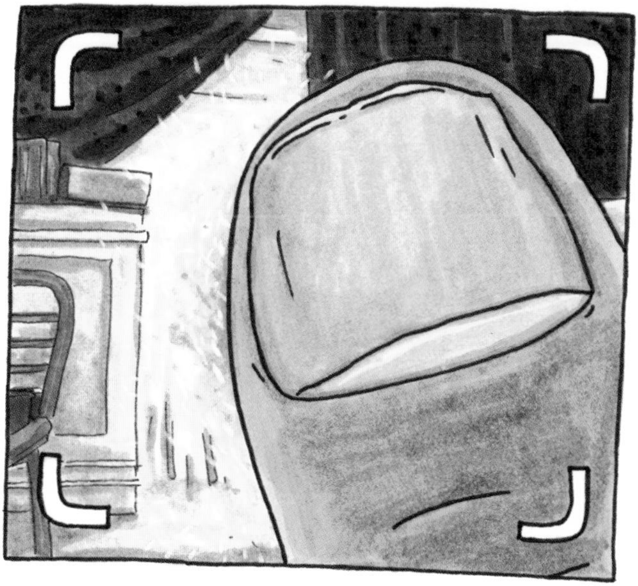

TITHONUS

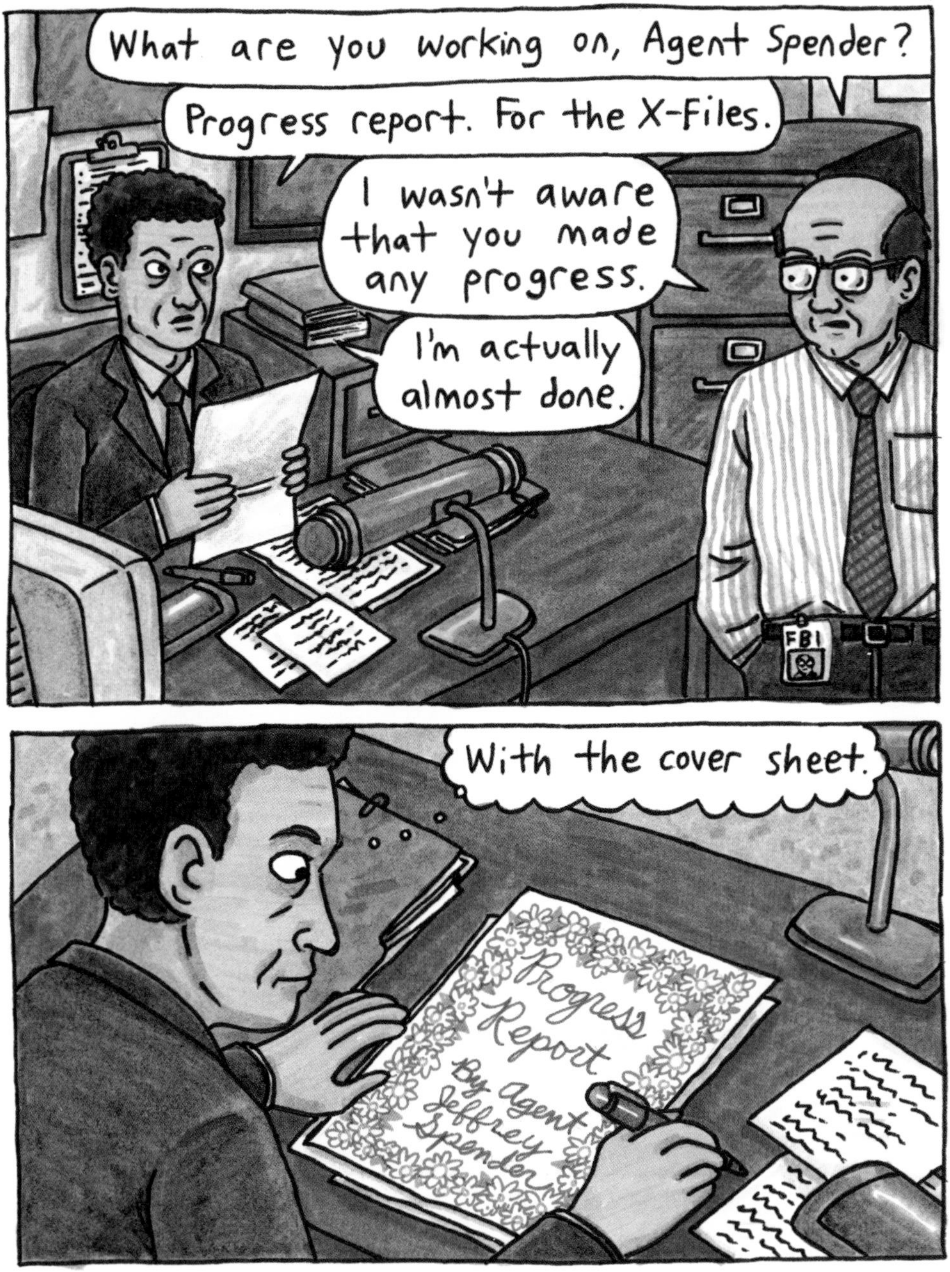
What are you working on, Agent Spender?
Progress report. For the X-Files.
I wasn't aware that you made any progress.
I'm actually almost done.
With the cover sheet.
Progress Report
By agent Jeffrey Spender
FBI

TWO FATHERS

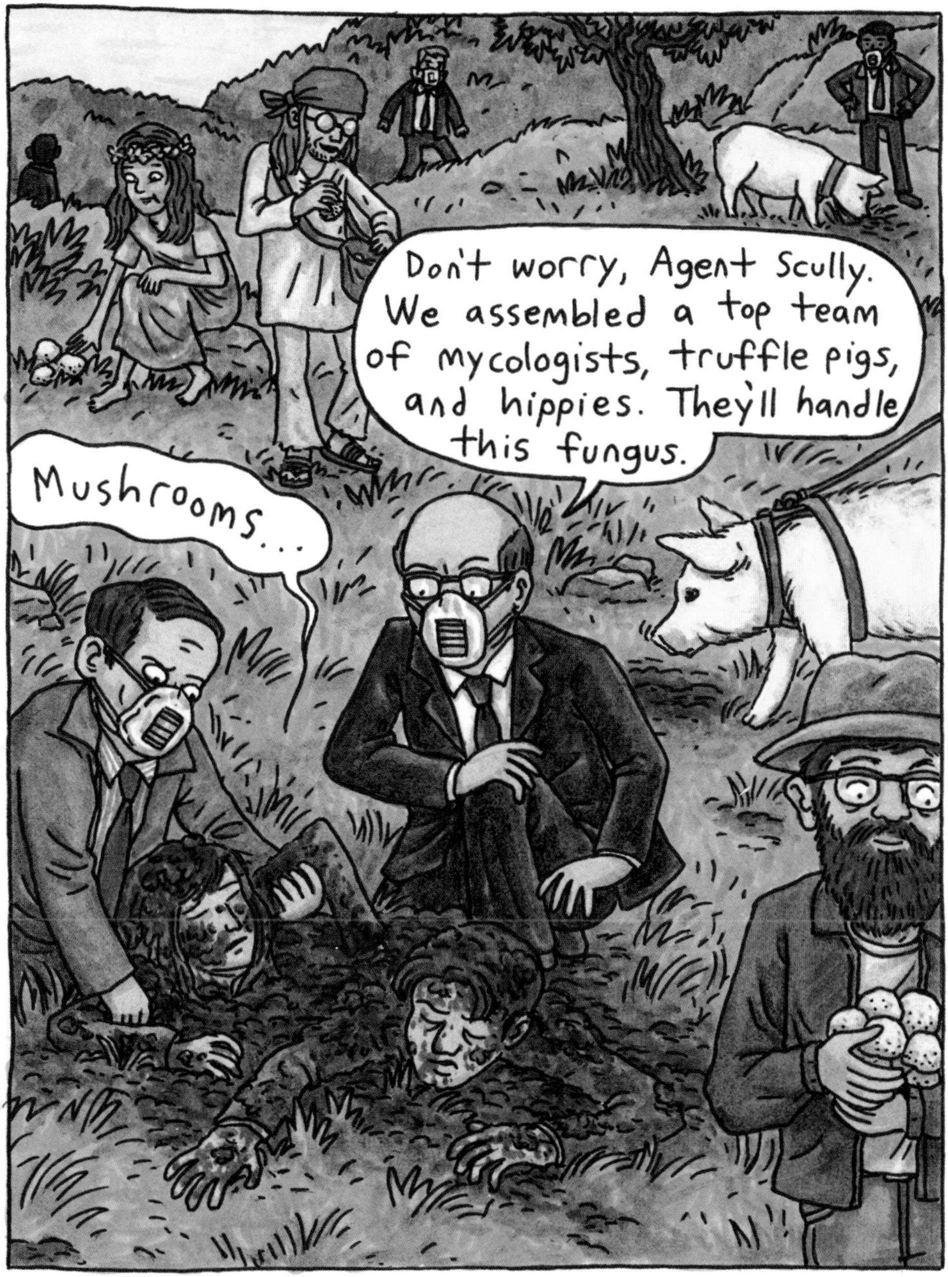
Don't worry, Agent Scully. We assembled a top team of mycologists, truffle pigs, and hippies. They'll handle this fungus.
Mushrooms...

FIELD TRIP

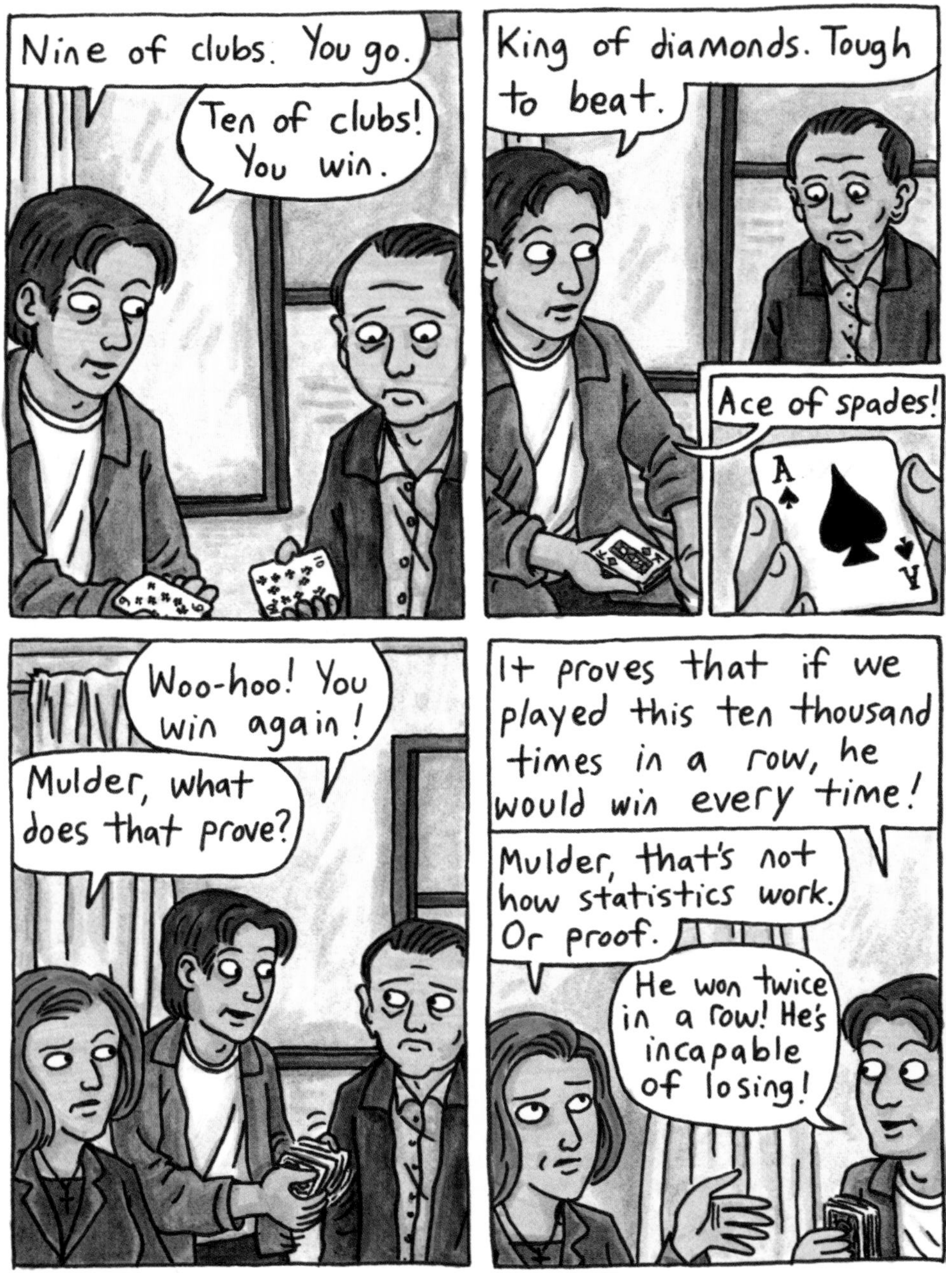
Nine of clubs. You go.
Ten of clubs! You win.
King of diamonds. Tough to beat.
Ace of spades!
A
Woo-hoo! You win again!
Mulder, what does that prove?
It proves that if we played this ten thousand times in a row, he would win every time!
Mulder, that's not how statistics work. Or proof.
He won twice in a row! He's incapable of losing!

THE GOLDBERG VARIATION

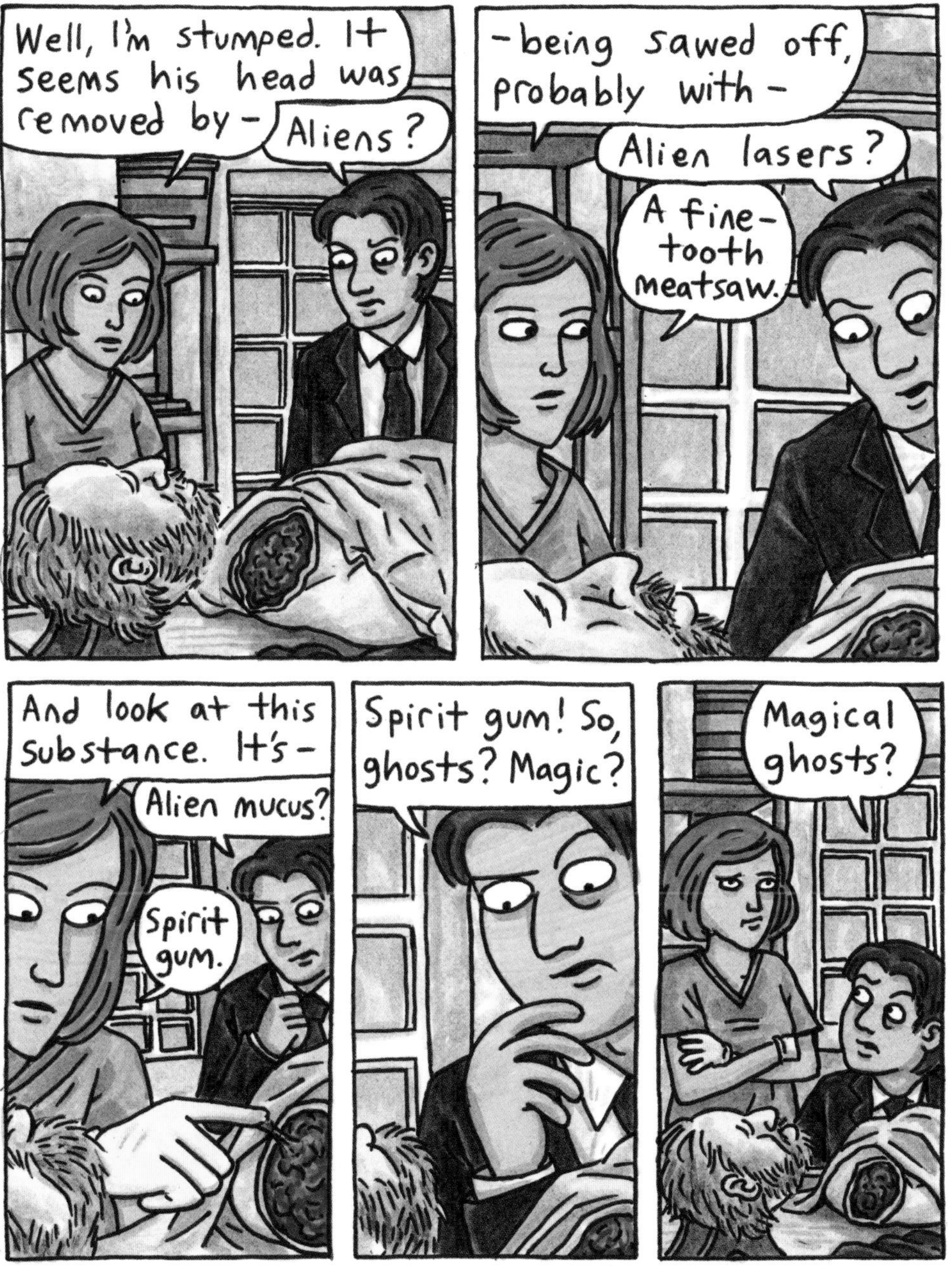
Well, I'm stumped. It seems his head was removed by—
Aliens?
—being sawed off, probably with—
Alien lasers?
A fine-tooth meatsaw.
And look at this substance. It's—
Alien mucus?
Spirit gum.
Spirit gum! So, ghosts? Magic?
Magical ghosts?

THE AMAZING MALEENI

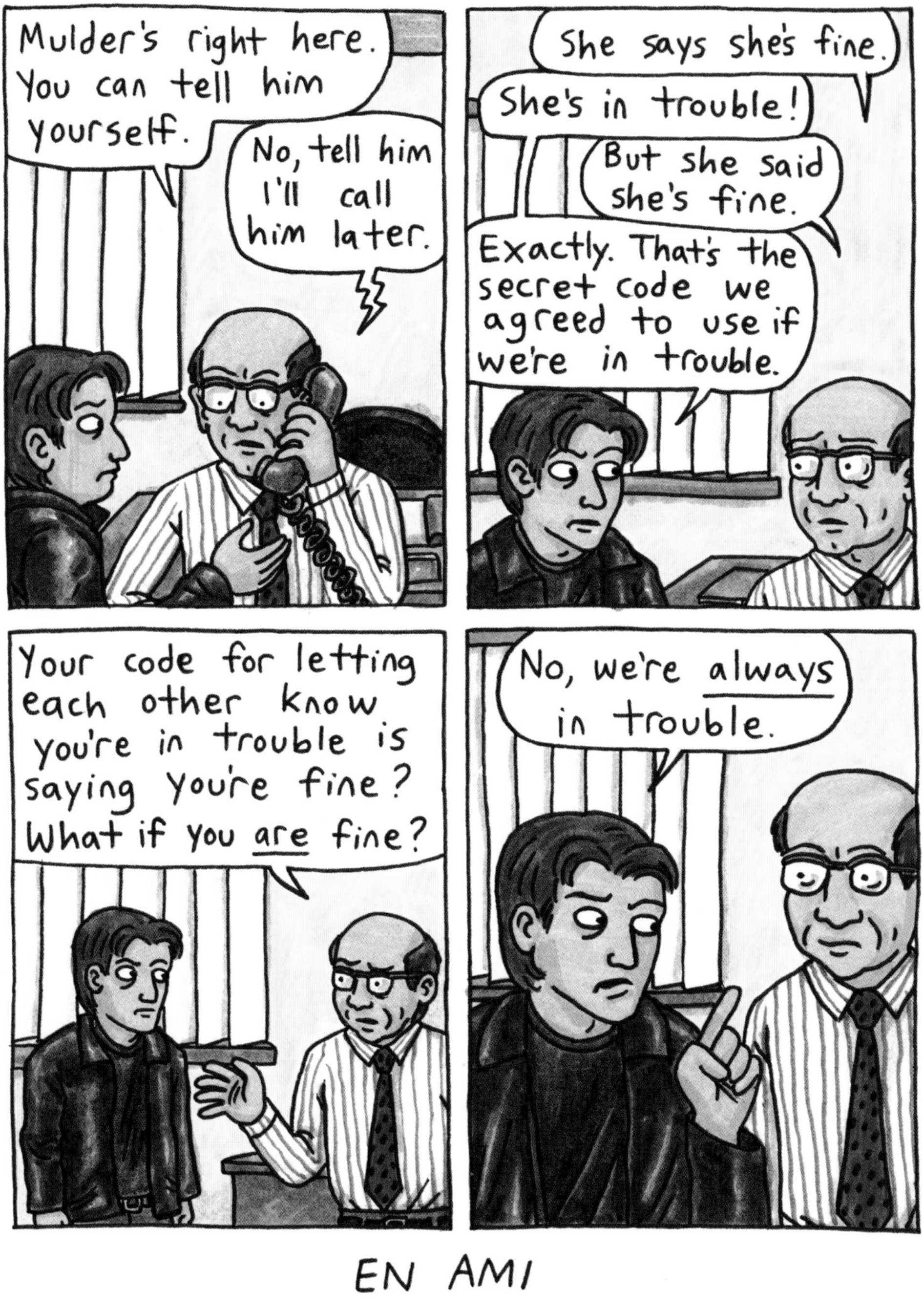
Mulder's right here. You can tell him yourself.
No, tell him I'll call him later.
She says she's fine.
She's in trouble!
But she said she's fine.
Exactly. That's the secret code we agreed to use if we're in trouble.
Your code for letting each other know you're in trouble is saying you're fine? What if you are fine?
No, we're always in trouble.

EN AMI

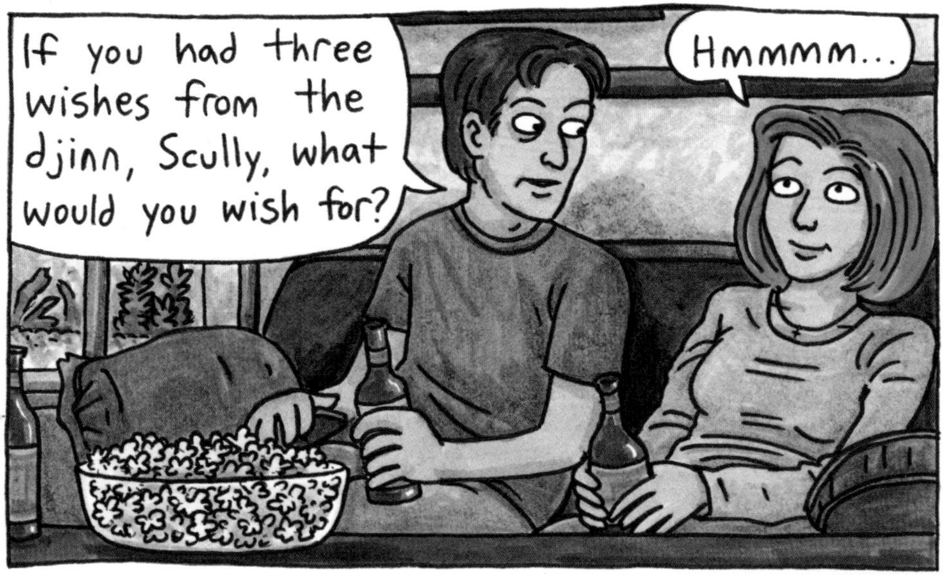
If you had three wishes from the djinn, Scully, what would you wish for?
Hmmmm...

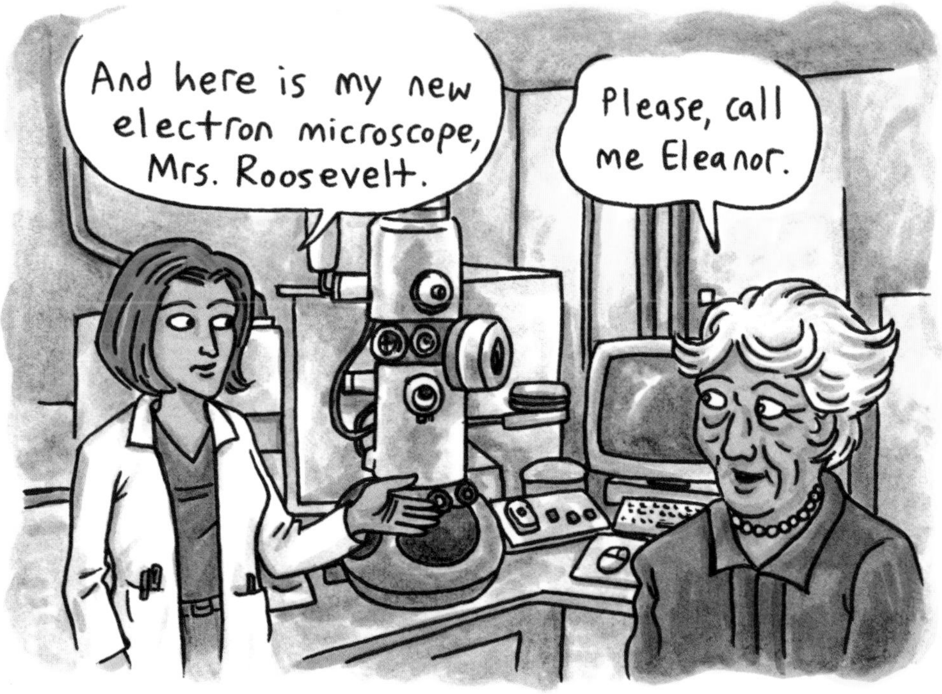
And here is my new electron microscope, Mrs. Roosevelt.
Please, call me Eleanor.

JE SOUHAITE

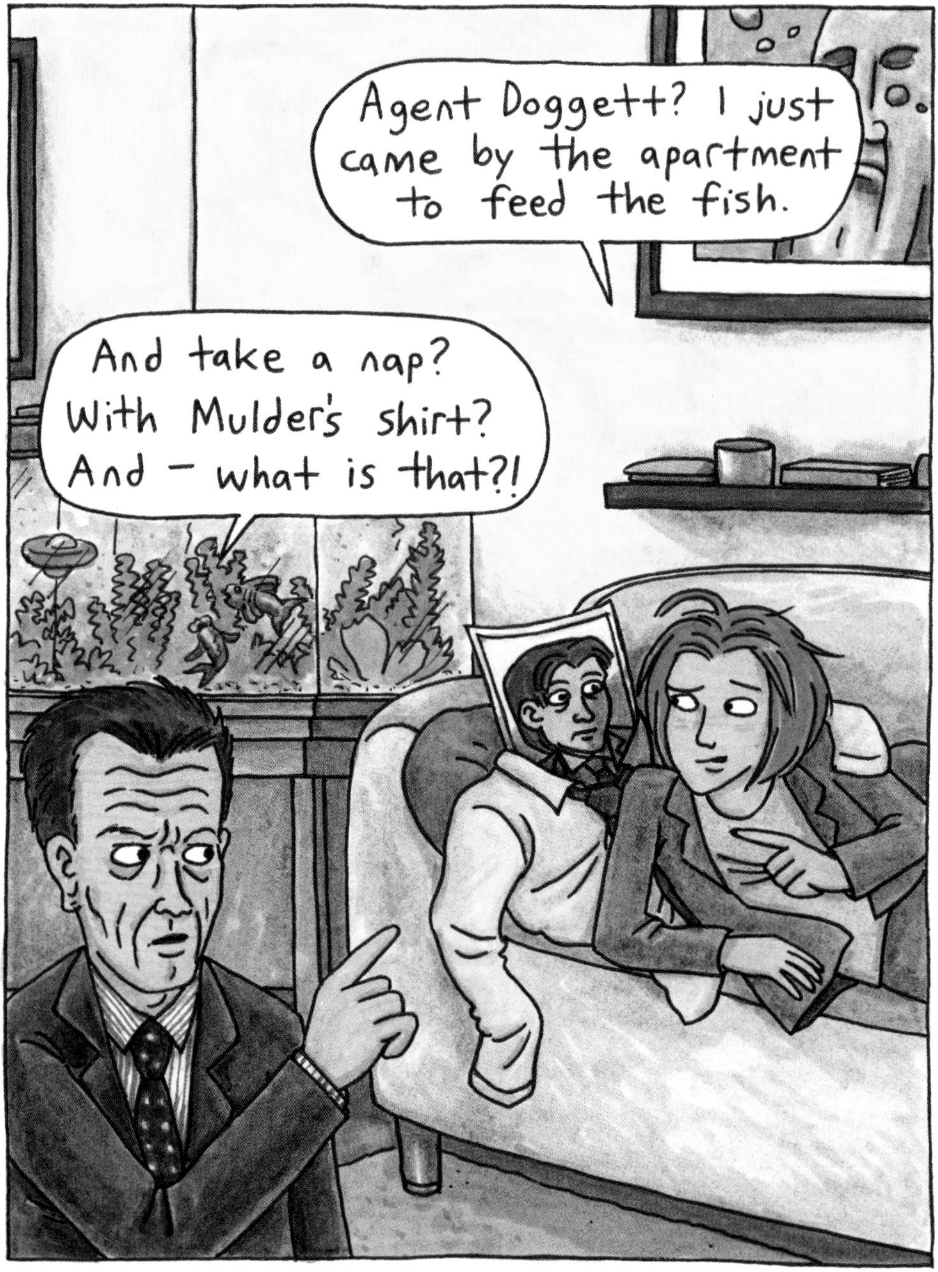
Agent Doggett? I just came by the apartment to feed the fish.
And take a nap? With Mulder's shirt? And - what is that?!

WITHIN

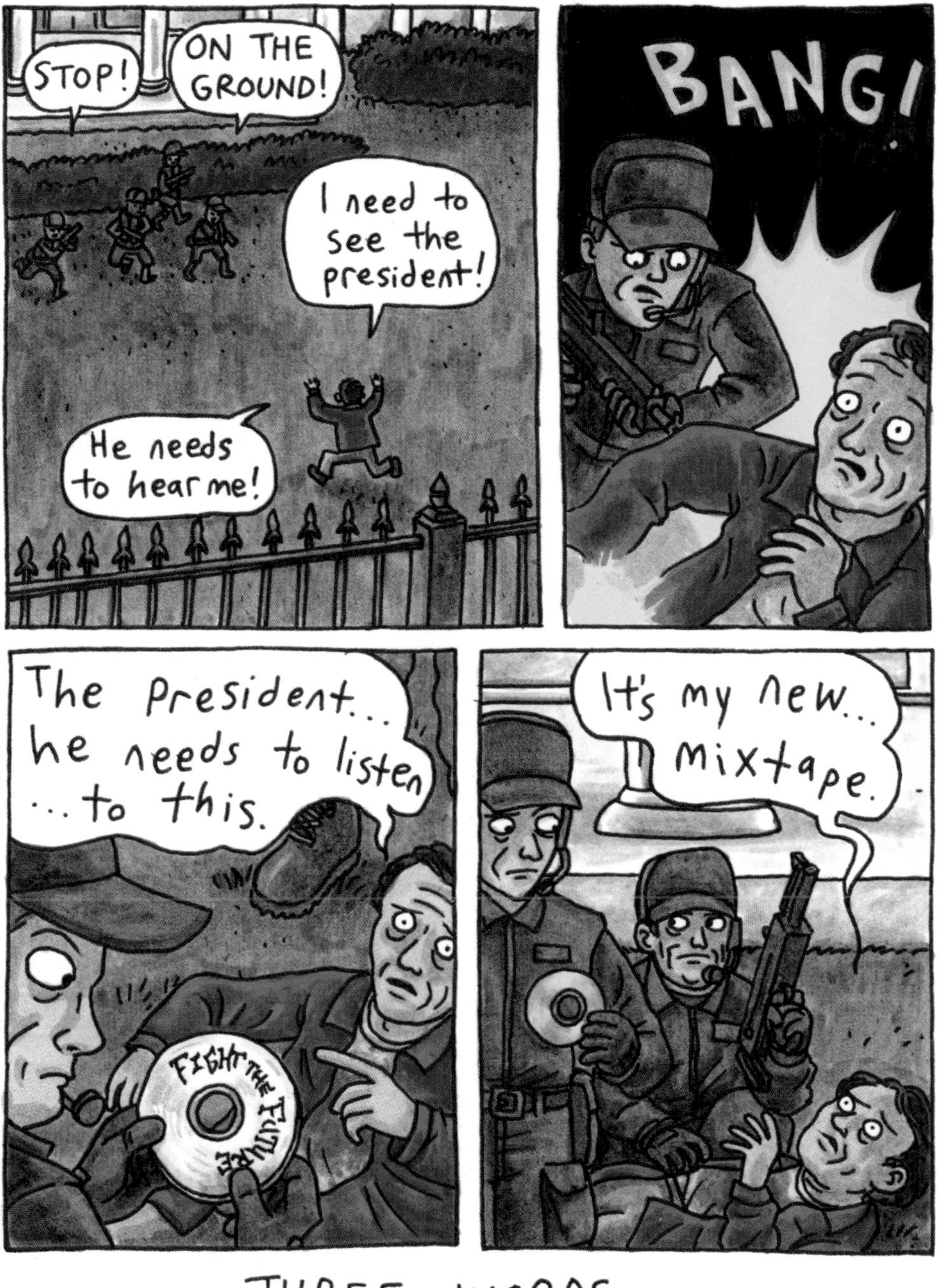
STOP!
ON THE GROUND!
I need to see the president!
He needs to hear me!
BANG!
The president... he needs to listen ...to this.
FIGHT THE FUTURE
It's my new... mixtape.

THREE WORDS

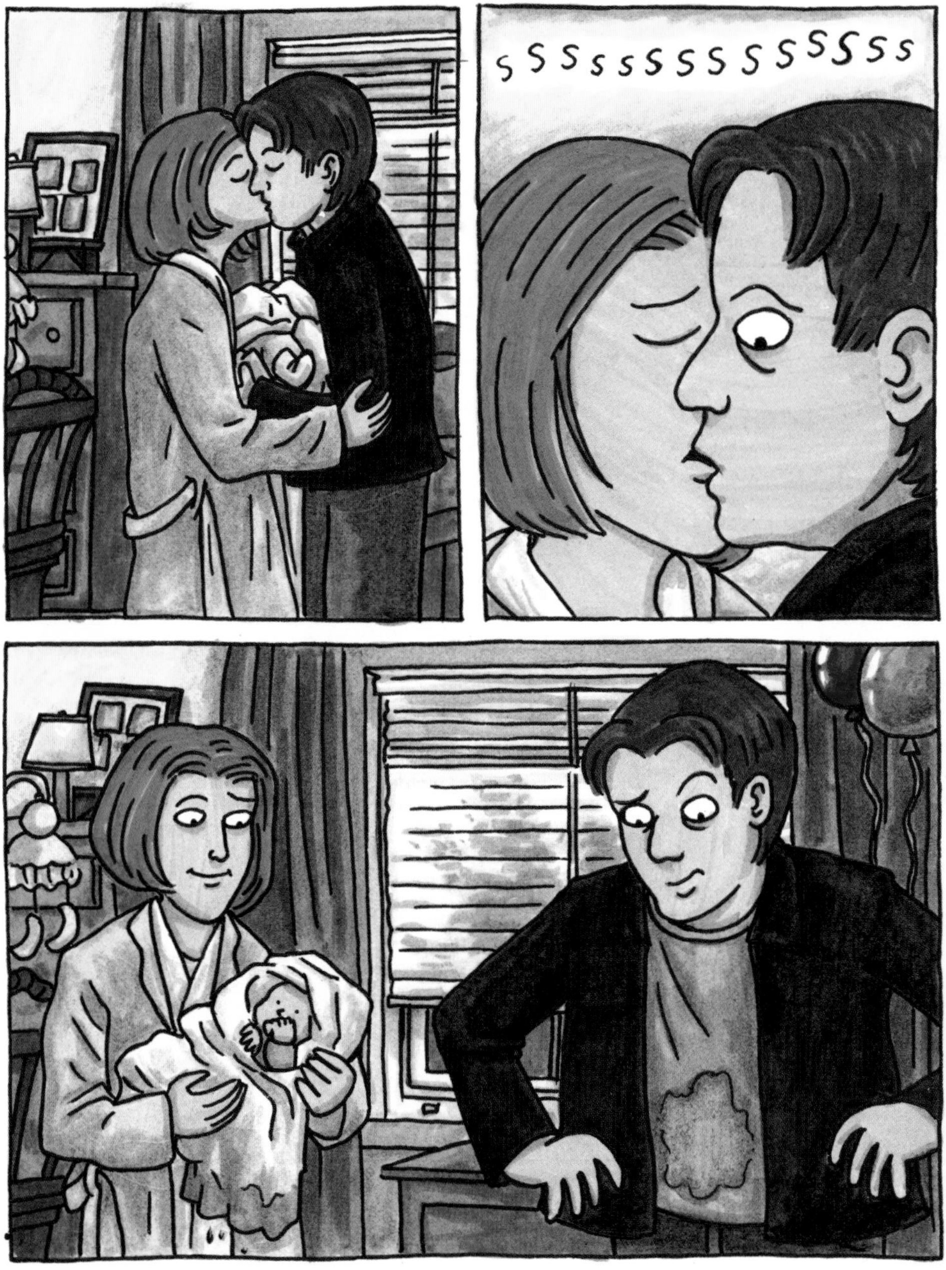
sssssssssssssss

EXISTENCE

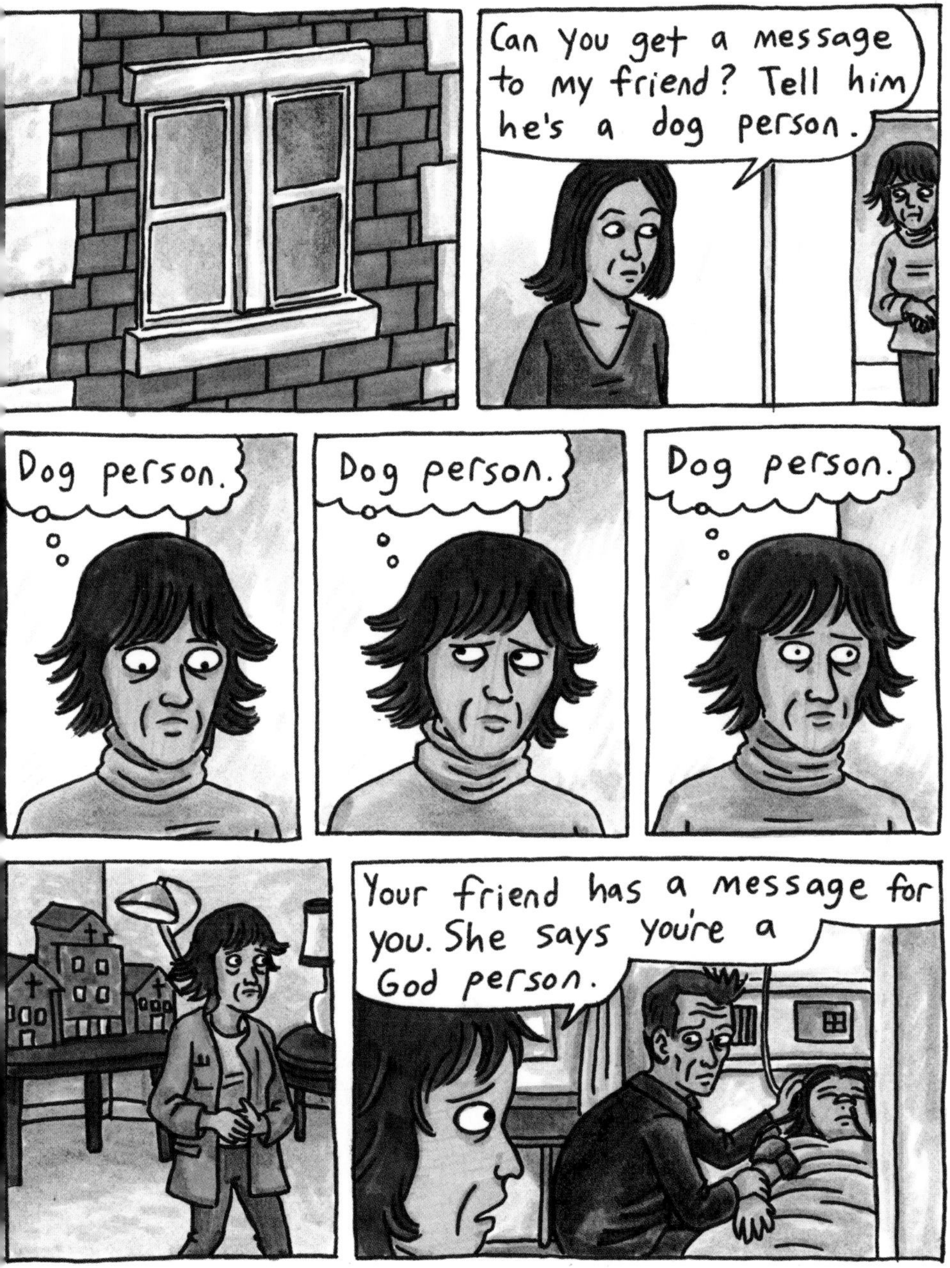
Can you get a message to my friend? Tell him he's a dog person.
Dog person.
Dog person.
Dog person.
Your friend has a message for you. She says you're a God person.

AUDREY PAULEY

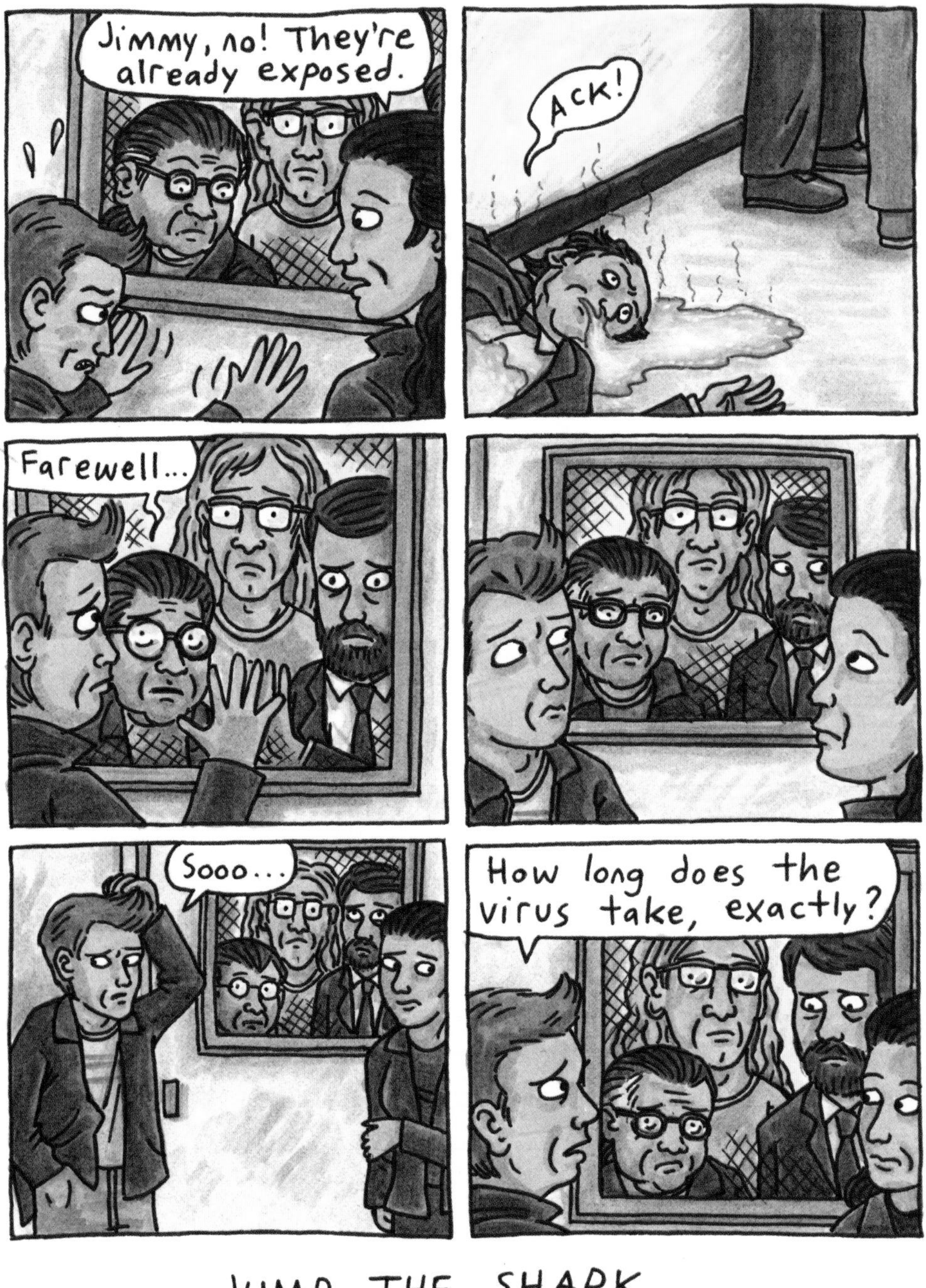
Jimmy, no! They're already exposed.
ACK!
Farewell...
Sooo...
How long does the virus take, exactly?

JUMP THE SHARK

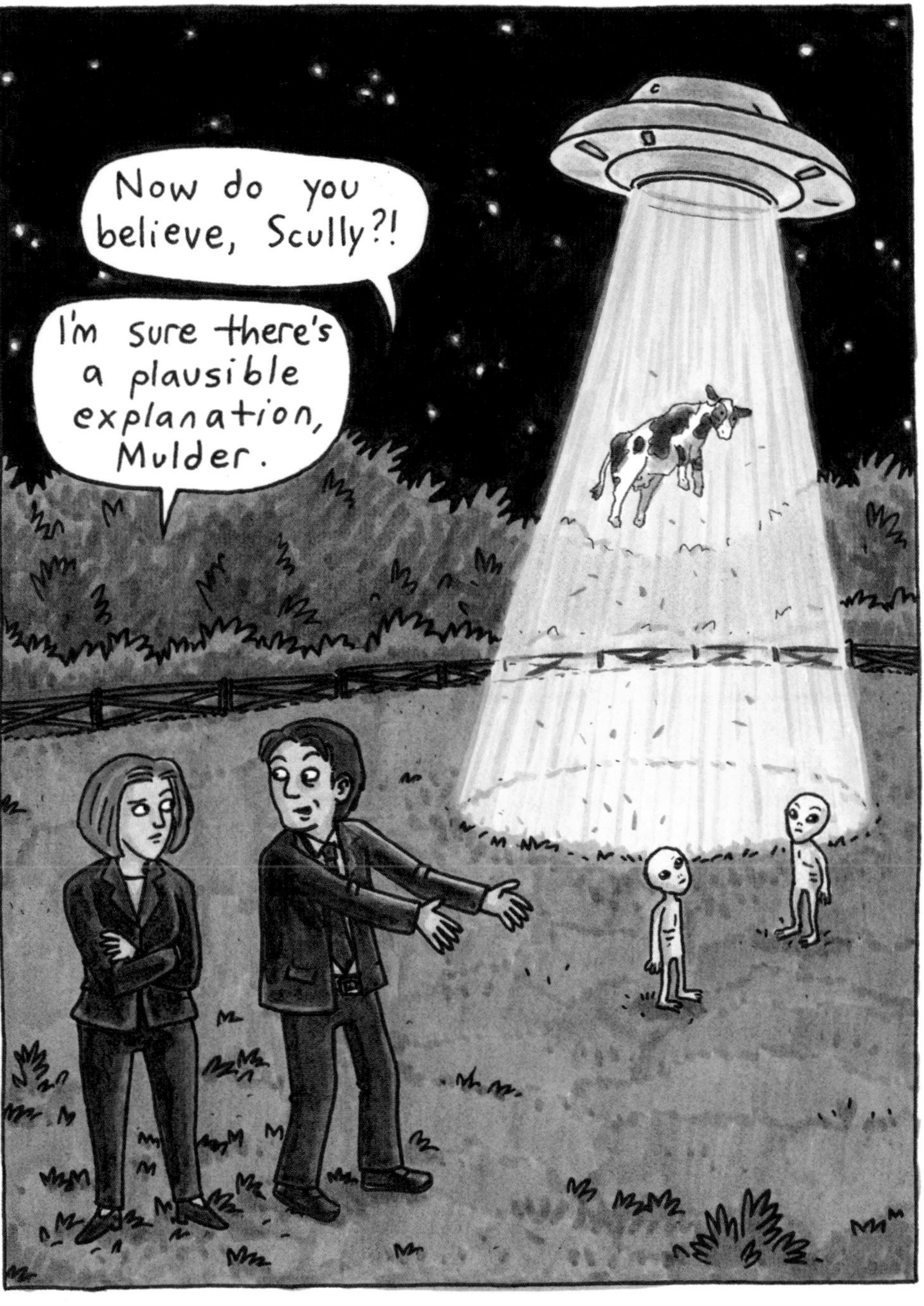
Now do you believe, Scully?!
I'm sure there's a plausible explanation, Mulder.

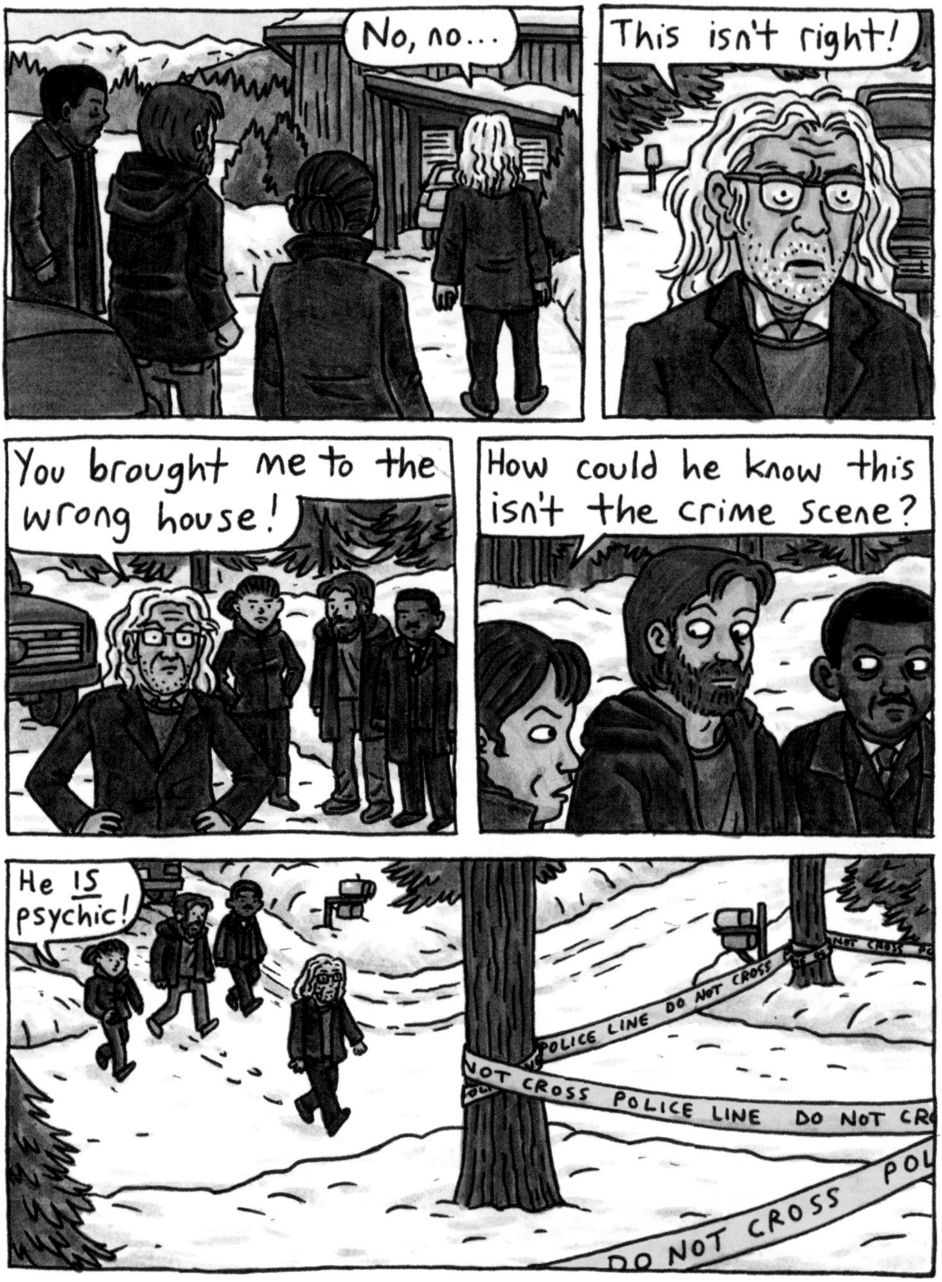
No, no...
This isn't right!
You brought me to the wrong house!
How could he know this isn't the crime scene?
He IS psychic!
POLICE LINE DO NOT CROSS
NOT CROSS POLICE LINE DO NOT CR
DO NOT CROSS POL

I WANT TO BELIEVE

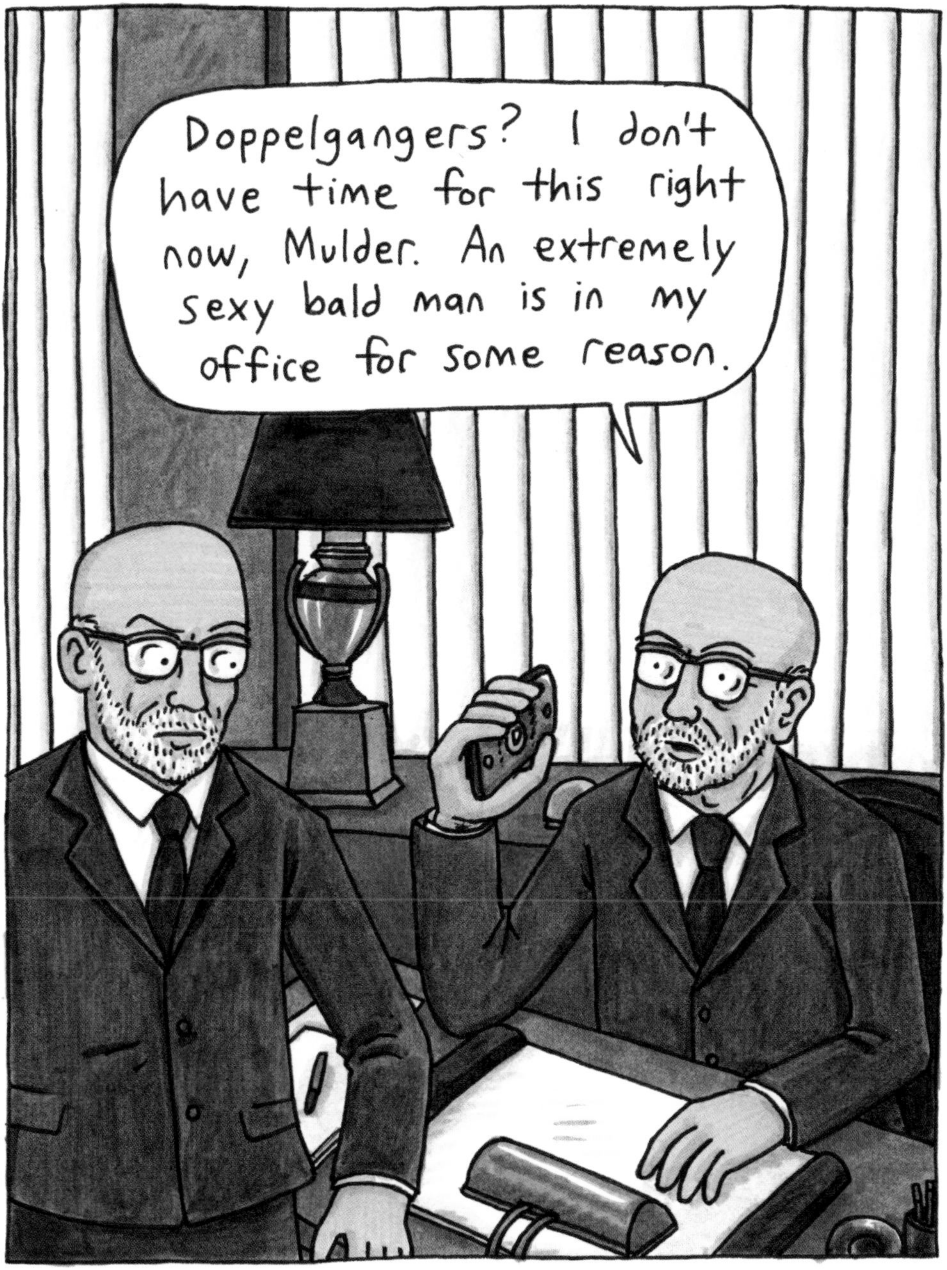
Doppelgangers? I don't have time for this right now, Mulder. An extremely sexy bald man is in my office for some reason.

PLUS ONE

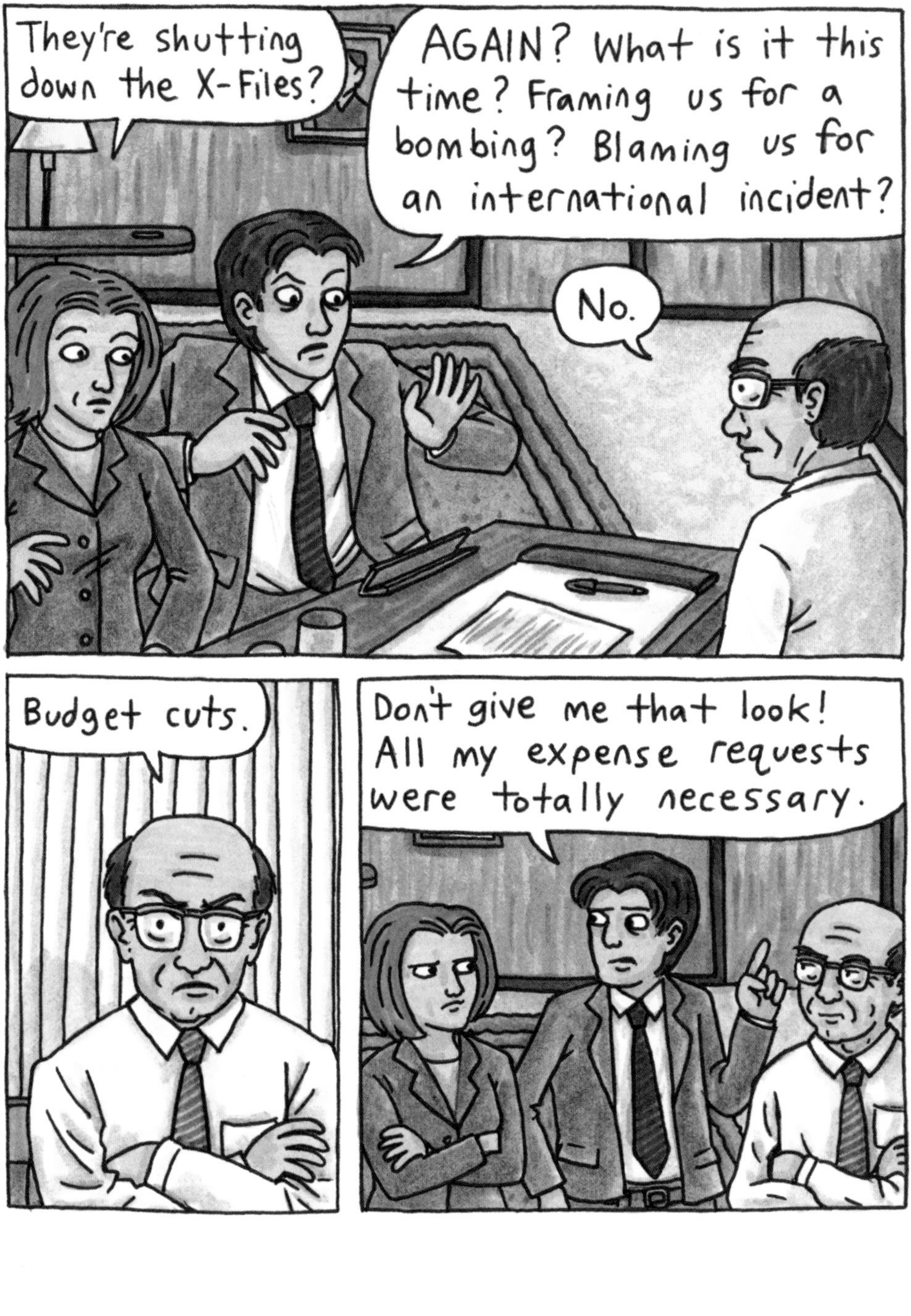
They're shutting down the X-Files?
AGAIN? What is it this time? Framing us for a bombing? Blaming us for an international incident?
No.
Budget cuts.
Don't give me that look! All my expense requests were totally necessary.

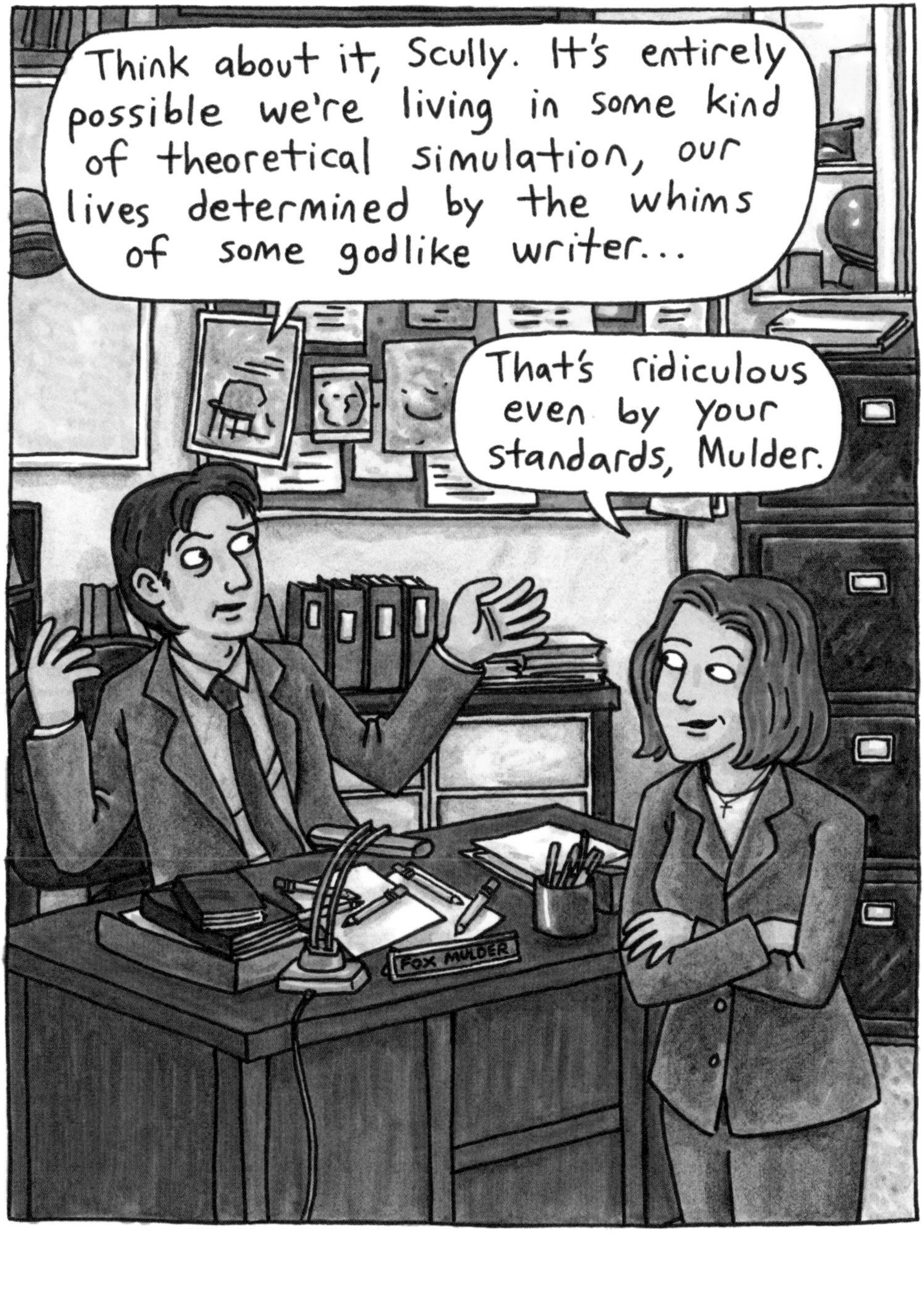
Think about it, Scully. It's entirely possible we're living in some kind of theoretical simulation, our lives determined by the whims of some godlike writer...
That's ridiculous even by your standards, Mulder.
FOX MULDER

ABOUT THE AUTHOR

JEFFREY BROWN

SUBJECT IS A CARTOONIST KNOWN FOR THE BESTSELLING *DARTH VADER AND SON* SERIES AND NUMEROUS OTHER GRAPHIC NOVELS. BROWN ATTENDED THE SAME HIGH SCHOOL IN GRAND RAPIDS, MICHIGAN, AS ACTRESS GILLIAN ANDERSON, WHO PORTRAYED AGENT DANA SCULLY ON *THE X-FILES.* COINCIDENCE... OR CONSPIRACY?!

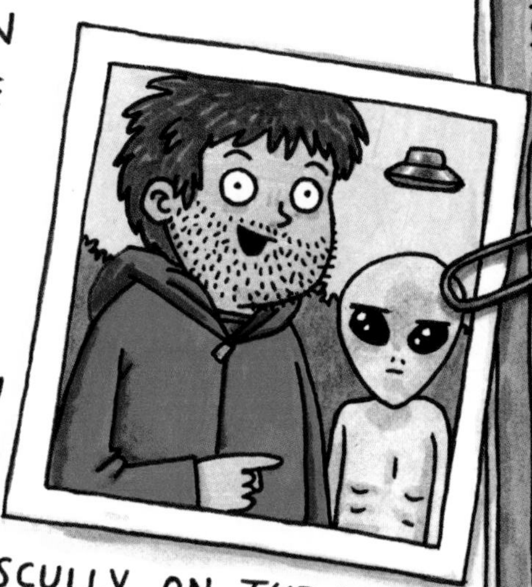

JEFFREYBROWNCOMICS.COM
PO BOX 120
DEERFIELD, IL 60015-0120
USA

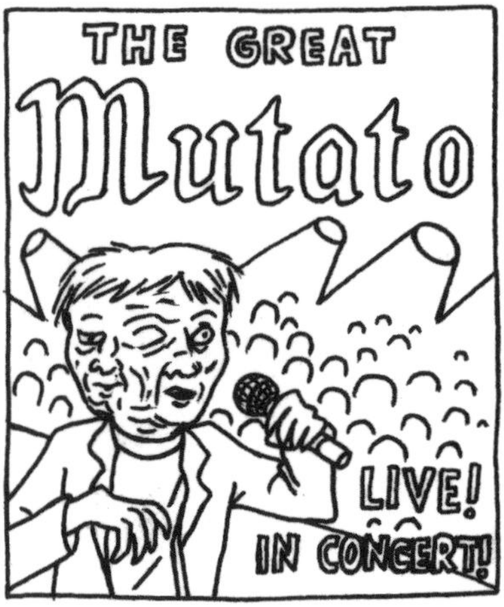
THE GREAT
Mutato
LIVE!
IN CONCERT!

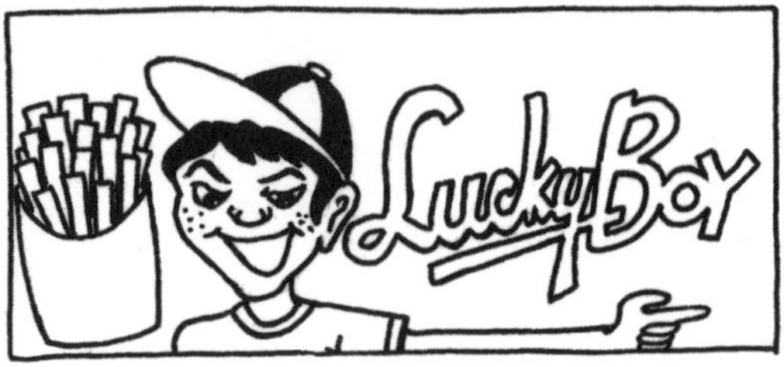
Lucky Boy

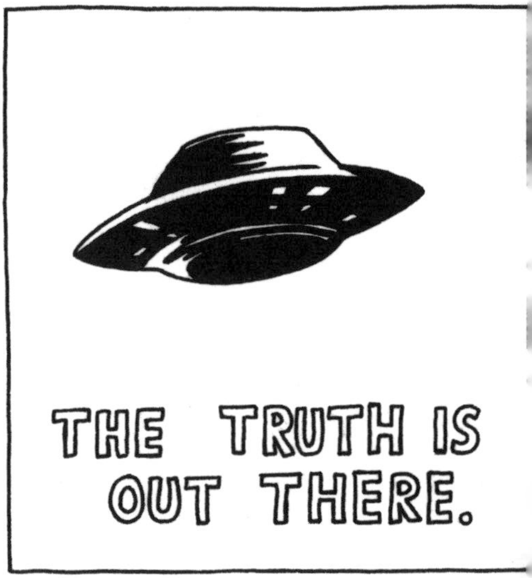
THE TRUTH IS OUT THERE.

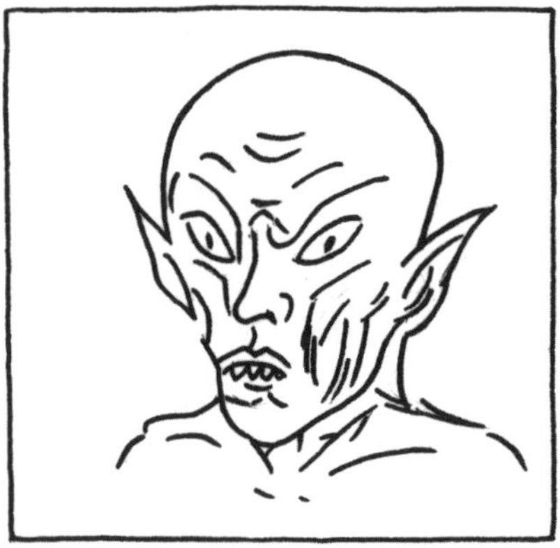

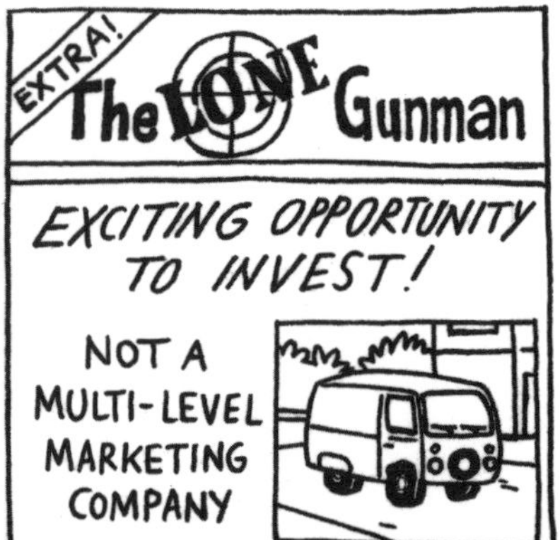
EXTRA!
The LONE Gunman
EXCITING OPPORTUNITY TO INVEST!
NOT A MULTI-LEVEL MARKETING COMPANY

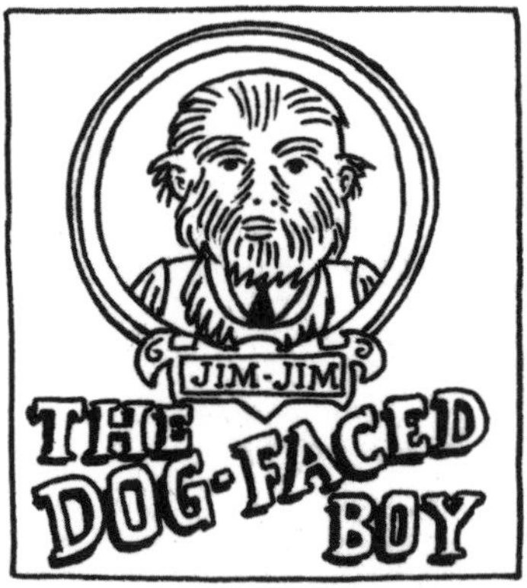
JIM-JIM
THE DOG-FACED BOY

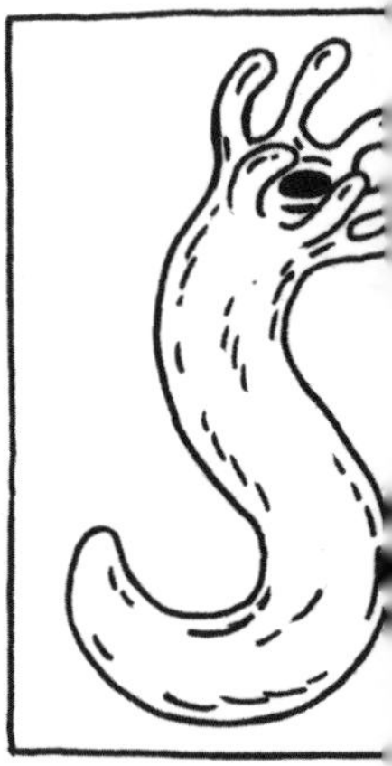